MURDER

AT THE PONY SHOW

An Irish murder mystery with a killing,
a kidnap, and a lot of other horseplay

DAVID PEARSON

THE
BOOK
FOLKS

D1581244

Paperback edition published by

The Book Folks

London, 2018

ISBN 978-1-7181-5596-1

www.thebookfolks.com

To Graham and Gillian, for their encouragement and support.

Prologue

The Connemara Pony Show takes place every year in Clifden, County Galway. It's a well-attended affair, with enthusiasts coming from all over Europe and even some from North America, to trade in these fine animals, or even just to admire the elegant, good humoured ponies, unique to this part of the west of Ireland.

The show is usually scheduled for the third week of August so as not to clash with the much bigger equine event in Dublin at the start of the month. The show used to mark the end of the tourist season in the region, but latterly, thanks to the promotion of the Wild Atlantic Way, tourists continue to visit Clifden and its surroundings well into the Autumn.

The Connemara pony is an animal that normally stands between thirteen and fifteen hands high. They have largely been reared in the boggy, rocky terrain west and north west of Galway, and due to the weather in those parts they are very hardy animals. They are sociable beasts and can often be seen grazing in twos or threes on the meagre grass that characterizes the area in all weathers. Commonly either light grey or bay in colour, they are quite easy to train, and have become favoured as an excellent starter horse for young riders, and girls in particular.

The show itself features competition of all kinds in many categories, and of course buying and selling of the ponies is commonplace. The prices paid for a good breeding mare with some pedigree are not enormous – rarely more than a few thousand euro, although at one of the shows in recent years a pony fetched over €20,000 when it was sold to a Swiss buyer, a record which has been talked about ever since. Most of the owners and breeders are not in it for the money, but rather for the love of the animals, and the breed in general, and the camaraderie and friendly competitions that ensue.

The show attracts not just the pony set, but a lot of other transient visitors as well. There are the inevitable food stalls selling everything from organic yoghurt smoothies to greasy burgers; the tack stalls that take up a generous corner of the show ground with their saddles, bridles, riding hats and other specialized gear, and of course a mobile bar dispensing over-priced beer and stout to the thirsty show-goers.

All of these people have to be accommodated for the week. The hotels are normally fully booked several months in advance, and often put their prices up as much as they dare, knowing that beds will fetch a healthy premium at this particular time. There are scores of Bed and Breakfast places too. These are either terraced houses lining the wide streets of Clifden itself, or bungalows dotted around the nearby countryside, where the owners have given over two or three bedrooms to guests. Airbnb, a new phenomenon on the scene, has also become very active, and hosts who would struggle at any other time of year for a booking, find themselves bombarded with requests for what could be quite modest accommodation.

The catchment zone for visitors to the show covers a large area. For those who care not for frugality, the magnificent Ballynahinch Castle plays host to the elite and well-heeled attendees, some of whom take advantage of the hotel's famous salmon fishery on the river that meanders through its extensive estate. The castle marks the eastern boundary of the footprint for the pony show. Between there and Letterfrack on the northern side of Clifden, and taking in Roundstone, Ballyconneely and Clifden itself, hostelries of all shapes and sizes soak up the throng, with any stragglers who have been tardy with their arrangements having to settle for Galway or Westport, each over an hour's drive away.

Chapter One

By 8:30 a.m. on Wednesday, the second day of the pony show, things were beginning to get busy at the grounds. The stables were being cleaned out, and for those participants who had not been able to reserve a loose box, and had to overnight the animals in their own towable trailers, there was much work to be done.

Today there would be jumping for riders under sixteen years of age in the arena, and then later on a dressage competition would take place with the ponies and riders showing off their prowess with the animals high stepping, walking diagonally across the arena known as "Piaffe" in the jargon, trotting and cantering, and even walking backwards. Dressage is designed to show the audience manoeuvres that are not natural for a large four-legged animal, and requires months and months of meticulous training and a very strong bond of understanding between horse and rider.

Following the dressage, prizes were to be awarded for the best turned out pony and rider, a coveted reward that generally went to one of the junior competitors who might have spent hours preparing their mounts just for the occasion. The day finished up with the presentation of a large silver plate for the overall best in show combination.

Jenny Gillespie was enjoying the show, much as she had done for the past three years. Now fifteen, she was old enough and big enough to manage her beautiful bay Connemara Pony, but still young enough to compete in junior competitions.

Her pony, whose registered name was Errigal Maiden, was known generally as "Lady". Lady stood thirteen hands in height and her pale beige coat nicely contrasted with a dark brown main and tail in the classic Connemara style. The animal had a gentle disposition, which had been a major factor in its selection when Jenny's father, Cathal, had bought the pony for his daughter four years previously. Cathal ran a very successful light engineering business on the outskirts of Donegal town. The company manufactured harrows and grass cutting equipment, and bespoke machinery for some of the many small industries dotted around Sligo and Donegal, as well as metal road trailers, and rather strangely, frames for mobility scooters.

The Gillespie household occupied a substantial two storey house a few miles outside Donegal Town on five acres of land adjacent to Lough Eske. Apart from the five-bedroomed dwelling, Cathal had erected a large metal workshop close to the property where he stored his beloved classic Mark II Jaguar, and another building that was comprised of two separate stables, a tack room, a sluice room and a feed store, all tastefully finished and maintained in good condition.

Jenny had competed in many events since getting her pony, and had often been successful, bringing home a trophy, or at least a small collection of rosettes, which she had pinned up all around Lady's stable. She was hoping to add to the haul at this year's show, and was particularly looking forward to the dressage, at which both she and Lady excelled.

* * *

When the Gillespies arrived at the show ground that morning, just a short drive from where they were staying at the Abbey Glen Hotel, Jenny made straight for Lady's horsebox to start the day's routine. She opened the small front door of the trailer and entered, saying hello to her pony, who seemed, unusually, to be somewhat agitated. Jenny stroked the horse's neck and snout, and uttered soothing words, but Lady continued to scratch the floor with her front hoof and whinnied and neighed uncomfortably, tossing her head back and forth. Jenny moved down alongside the animal, thinking that maybe its hind legs were caught up in something.

At first Jenny couldn't believe what she was looking at, but there, at the back of the horsebox, jammed between her pony's back legs and the rear door, was the body of a man, the back of his head caked in blood. Jenny managed to get back out of the horsebox before letting out a spine-chilling scream, and then another, and another, drawing attention from the other competitors around and about and of course from her father who was sitting in their car at the edge of the arena reading emails on his phone.

Cathal rushed over to his daughter and enveloped her in his arms, stroking her hair, and saying, "It's all right precious, it's all right, what's the matter?"

Jenny was sobbing uncontrollably and couldn't speak, but she was able to point to the trailer, and another man standing nearby who had witnessed her outburst went to investigate. Several other owners had come across to Lady's trailer hearing the commotion, and it wasn't long before the horror of the situation was revealed to the small crowd. Cathal Gillespie wasted no time in taking control of things. He asked one of the men to go to the entrance of the show ground and fetch a policeman.

For the three days of the pony show, four extra uniformed Gardaí had been drafted into Clifden. Two worked the 8:00 a.m. to 2:00 p.m. shift, and the other two took over at 2:00 and worked through to 8:00 p.m. by which time the activity at the show ground had petered out. A private security firm was then employed to watch the place overnight, so that the valuable equipment and ponies could be secured.

When the man had been despatched to find a Garda, Cathal said to the others, "We have to get Lady out of there. Will someone open the back door of the horsebox, gently now, and I'll see if Jenny can get her out without making matters worse."

The tailgate of the box, fortunately a double width affair, was gently lowered and as it came open the legs of the dead man fell outwards, so that the body was half in and half out of the contraption.

Jenny, who had managed to get a grip on herself in the interests of the pony's wellbeing, entered the box again through the front door, and with some soothing talk slowly reversed Lady out of the trailer and down the ramp onto the concrete yard. While this was going on, Cathal ensured that the corpse was protected from any further damage. Jenny led her pony away. It had been agreed that she could be housed in one of the permanent stables that had been allocated to another pony who would be put out into the paddock to make room.

Once Lady was away from the dead man, she calmed down a little, but Jenny insisted on staying with her, comforting her. The animal had had a bad shock.

* * *

Garda Michael Costello was first to attend the scene.

"Jesus, what in God's name has happened here?" he said.

Cathal explained what had taken place when his daughter had first arrived to tend to her pony.

"And who's bright idea was it to move the animal? You know this could be a crime scene!" Costello said.

"We didn't have a choice. If we had left the pony in there she could have easily trampled on him. She was quite distressed," Cathal explained.

"We'll see about that," Costello said, turning away to call the matter in to Clifden Garda station where Sergeant Séan Mulholland was just opening up for the day.

Mulholland was in his mid-fifties, and could have retired from the Garda Síochána by now, but being a solitary bachelor with few outside interests other than a bit of coarse fishing, he had stayed on, enjoying the camaraderie afforded by the job, which for the most part was not too taxing. He was a tall man, standing a full six foot, with a good crop of greying hair, a ruddy face, and a substantial, but not obese, build. He spent most of his time keeping the Garda station in Clifden running smoothly, renewing shotgun licenses for the farmers in the area, and filling out endless, and as he saw it, largely pointless forms for the regional administration based in Galway. A man of habit, when he had finished his shift each day, he would retire to Cusheen's Bar in the main street for three or four pints and a read of the paper before heading home to his rather drab cottage out on the Skye Road.

"God, that's all we need, Michael. Can you tape off the area all around the horsebox and see that it's not disturbed? Don't let anyone touch anything, and don't let anyone leave. Any idea what might have happened?" Mulholland said.

"Dunno, sarge. Looks like the deceased may have got into the trailer for a kip – maybe he was pissed – and the pony kicked him to death, but I can't be sure," Costello said.

"OK. Well you and McGrath do your best for now. I'll get the other two out to you as soon as I can, and I'll have to call this in to Galway. Yer man is definitely dead, is he? No point in calling an ambulance?" Mulholland said.

"No, sarge, no point at all."

Chapter Two

Mrs Cathleen Curley, together with her husband John, were the proprietors of the Ocean View Guesthouse, located between Ballyconneely and Clifden. It certainly lived up to its name with a fantastic view of the ocean looking out over Ballyconneely Bay with its deep blue, almost aquamarine, sea and bright yellow patches of beach dotted along the coastline. The house stood well back from the road with a neatly tarred driveway and adequate parking for four or five cars out in front. John had built the house himself soon after he married Cathleen, on land owned and worked by his father. His father was a quiet industrious man who had spent many years clearing the ten acres of rocky scrubland, taking out huge limestone boulders and digging deep drainage channels all around, so that now the smallholding was fertile enough to support a handful of beef cattle over the summer months. The income from the cattle and the guesthouse afforded the Curleys a comfortable, if not extravagant lifestyle, and they were proud of their two teenage children both of whom were attending University College Galway studying Agricultural Science and Marketing respectively.

Cathleen Curley was a large woman in every respect. Her frame was large, her personality, her voice and even her generosity and good cheer exceeded the norms of modern society by a fair measure. As a result, Cathleen progressed through life seeing few obstacles, and had used this unusual demeanour to build a nice little business where others might have struggled. Cathleen had three guest bedrooms at Ocean View that were built into the attic space of their bungalow. John had done the conversion with the help of a few friends from around the area when tourism began to blossom into a serious business in 2004. Ocean View enjoyed a very high occupancy rate from Easter right through to October, with many of the bookings coming by word of mouth, helped along by a string of excellent reviews on TripAdvisor. Unlike many hosts in the area, Cathleen didn't increase her rates for Show Week. She was happy with the yield her business provided, and she disliked the exploitation and greed exhibited by some of the other owners, but kept her views to herself.

John and herself had discussed extending the premises for the next season and had plans and drawings prepared by a local architect. John had approached Galway County Council who were amenable to the idea of a dormer styled extension to the side of the house that would provide additional bedrooms, a large sitting room with views out to sea, and a dining room capable of seating all of their guests. The Council were keen to encourage an increase in capacity in the area, and told John that there might even be a grant available to help with the cost.

* * *

In the week in question, Ocean View had three parties staying. In room one, Eileen and Shane Farley from Carlow had booked for the whole week. The Farleys kept horses on their own land at home, and combined their annual trip to the pony show with a short holiday in the beautiful countryside in the west of Ireland. Using Ocean View as their base, on days when they weren't going to the show, they would drive out through Letterfrack and on out to Louisburgh and Leenaun. On these days, Cathleen would insist on giving the Farleys a pack lunch comprised of ham and tomato sandwiches, generous slices of home baked cake, and an enormous flask of tea.

Room two was occupied by a couple from England. The Ashtons were keen followers of the Connemara breed, and spent as much time as they could at the show. They knew many of the breeders and competitors, and enjoyed watching the various events each day as the ponies went through their drills and exhibitions.

The occupant of room three was different. A single man, or at least travelling on his own, David Ellis was average in almost every respect. He was of average height, average weight, with an average appearance and average brown hair. His clothes were average too. He wore plain grey slacks, a check, button-down shirt and a sleeveless green pullover topped off with a Harris Tweed jacket. The only distinguishing feature of the man was the expensive digital SLR camera that could be seen in his company anytime he went outdoors.

Despite Cathleen's well-developed skill of subtly questioning her guests about every aspect of their lives, she had been singularly unsuccessful in discovering much about Ellis, who had insisted on paying the double rate for his double room, given the pressure on accommodation at that time. Beyond his name and address, which Cathleen had looked up on Google maps – to discover, to no great surprise, was an average apartment in the Dublin suburbs – she could establish nothing at all about the man. Neither Facebook nor LinkedIn revealed any information at all about Ellis, which was in itself a bit odd, but he had paid in advance for his stay, in cash, and was perfectly pleasant, so apart from the frustration of not being able to find out anything about him, Cathleen was happy to have him as their guest. All was going well, that is until Wednesday morning when matters took a strange turn.

* * *

Cathleen rose at 6:45 a.m. each morning when they had people staying. Breakfast was served between 7:30 and 9:30 on weekdays, and between 8:30 and 10:30 at the weekends at Ocean View. Most of the visitors appeared between eight and nine, and Cathleen was well prepared. Before the start of service she would lay out a cold buffet of fresh seasonal fruit, cereals of all kinds, and a large jug of fresh orange juice. When she had guests from Scandinavia or Germany, this would be complimented by cold meats and cheeses, and for French visitors, she always provided croissants and pain au chocolat. Most Irish and English guests opted for a cooked breakfast, and Cathleen's "full Irish" was a substantial feast of bacon, sausages, black pudding, mushrooms, fried eggs and beans accompanied by lots of freshly made toast and as much tea or coffee as any human could comfortably imbibe. Following such an indulgence, her guests could often survive right through to teatime without having to touch another morsel.

On this morning, the Ashtons and the Farleys appeared at almost the same time, and all four ordered the "full Irish", putting not a little strain on Cathleen's capacity in the kitchen. But she coped well and the two couples were duly served with their morning banquet in a timely and very cheerful manner.

"It's a lovely day for the show," Cathleen said as she presented her masterpieces to the guests, "not too hot for the ponies, but I think it will stay dry, thank God."

The breakfasts were consumed enthusiastically, with Cathleen appearing from time to time to offer more toast or fresh tea and coffee, and by shortly after nine o'clock, all four had departed to go about their business.

Cathleen busied herself clearing away the dirty crockery from the dining room and tidying the kitchen for the next half hour. She liked to have breakfast completely finished before Mrs Magee, her daily help, arrived at ten o'clock. Mrs Magee lived close by and cycled daily, whatever the weather, from her own home to Ocean View where she spent four hours each day changing the bed linen, vacuuming the rooms thoroughly, topping up the tea and coffee sachets in each room, cleaning the bathrooms, and tending to the laundry. Then she would iron the sheets and pillowcases from the previous day's endeavours and finish up by giving the entire downstairs a good dusting to remove any traces of ash that had come from the open turf fire that Cathleen lit in the lounge every evening regardless of the weather.

At eleven thirty, it was customary for Mrs Magee and Cathleen to sit down for a cup of coffee and some homemade cake or scones, and a good gossip about the current patrons of the little enterprise.

"What happened to your man in room three?" Mrs Magee asked when she had finished loading the two washing machines in the utility room.

"Oh, good God, I completely forgot about Mr Ellis. I was so busy with breakfast. He never came down," Cathleen said.

"Well you needn't worry. He won't be wanting breakfast," said Mrs Magee, "he's not in his room, and his bed hasn't been slept in either."

"God, that's strange. He must have met someone in the town, or maybe he had too much to drink or something. Sure he'll turn up looking sheepish later, wait till you see," Cathleen said.

Chapter Three

It was a fine sunny day in Galway when Inspector Maureen Lyons got to work at Mill Street. Lyons was part of a five-man team headed up by Senior Inspector Mick Hays, whom she also lived with as her partner out in Salthill. It was a slightly unconventional arrangement, but Superintendent Plunkett tolerated it, as long as it didn't interfere with their work, and to date, there was no evidence that it had.

Lyons had moved in with Hays when she had been promoted to Inspector following the successful conviction of an avaricious murderer a couple of years previously. It had been a difficult and complex case, and Lyons' powerful instincts and somewhat unusual methods had been largely responsible for solving the crime where a harmless old man had been murdered by his nephew for some Coca Cola shares worth a few hundred thousand euro.

She had held onto her flat down by the river in Galway city though, in case her relationship with Hays went sour, but that hadn't happened so far, and the flat was sublet to a uniformed Garda working at the same station. On the week in question, Hays was away on a training course in the UK. "Crime Detection in the Digital Age" was the name of the course, and Hays told her it was mildly interesting, but that Galway seemed to be well ahead of most of the others in their use of technology.

"There's an inspector here from Wales somewhere who seems totally baffled by the whole thing. I don't even think they have broadband at their station. When the instructor used the word 'Instagram' he asked him if he didn't mean 'telegram'," Hays told her during one of their nightly telephone calls.

"Are there any gorgeous girls on the course?" Lyons asked.

"There are only two women out of the twelve of us, and if you saw them you wouldn't be concerned, trust me," he said.

Hays' team in Galway had its own technology super sleuth in the form of Garda John O'Connor, a uniformed officer assigned to the unit. O'Connor was a gem when it came to digging into a suspect's information on Facebook or Snapchat, and there was very little he couldn't find out given a criminal's mobile phone or computer. He loved the work, and was often sought out by other squads to assist when some knotty technology challenge was presented.

Lyons was using the week to catch up on the ever-present mountain of paperwork that the job generated these days. In the evening she went to her yoga classes, and while missing Hays' company, she was glad of the chance to catch up with her girlfriends, who, she had to admit, she had been neglecting somewhat of late. Of course, they all teased her mercilessly about Hays, and persistently asked her if there was 'any news', but she took it in good spirits. At thirty-six years old she had resigned herself to not having children, and she and Hays had agreed on this unanimously, though occasionally she wondered if she really meant it.

She was putting the finishing touches to a sizeable statistical report on "Detectives' use of Overtime, Vehicles and other Resources", a quarterly behemoth that regional administration always wanted, but for what she wasn't quite sure, when the phone on her desk came to life.

"Inspector Lyons?"

She immediately recognised the voice of Sergeant Séan Mulholland.

"Good morning, Séan. What's up?"

Mulholland went on to explain the events of the morning.

"Can we close down the pony show, Séan?" Lyons said.

"God, Inspector, that would be very difficult. Think of the bad publicity. There's all sorts of events scheduled for the day, and it may just be an unfortunate accident after all. Can we not let it go ahead? I'll make sure the scene is preserved," he said.

"Very well. But it's essential that the pony from the horsebox is kept isolated, and doesn't go out onto grass. There will be forensic evidence to be collected. And seal off the whole area around the trailer. Don't let anyone move it. I'll be out as quickly as I can," Lyons said.

Lyons grabbed her jacket from the back of the chair, closed the folder containing the statistical report and headed out into the open plan.

"Sally, Eamon, I need you both with me. There's been a death out at the pony show in Clifden. Sally, will you take the squad car? Eamon, you're with me in mine. Let's go!"

Sally was a young Detective Garda that had started out as a civilian worker with the detective unit under Hays some three years ago. She liked the work, and with a little persuasion from Maureen Lyons and a lot of soul-searching, she had put herself forward to join the force properly, and qualified as a fully-fledged Garda with distinction from the training school in Tullamore. Hays had pulled a few strings and managed to draft her into the unit, and he was glad that he had. She was a smart girl, and fitted in well with the others on the team.

* * *

Jenny Gillespie had been joined by her mother in the stable where Lady had been put after she was removed from the horsebox. Jenny was still very upset, but she had busied herself making up a bucket of nuts with a bottle of Guinness in it for her pony, and she was re-assured by the fact that Lady seemed to be much calmer, and more like her usual self.

Outside the stable block, Cathal was talking to Oliver Weldon, secretary of the Connemara Pony Society, who had come down as soon as he found out about the incident.

"They're saying that your daughter's pony kicked the man to death, Cathal," Weldon said.

"I can't see it, Oliver. The animal has a lovely temperament. I don't think I've ever seen her lash out, not even with a dog snapping at her heels," Cathal said.

"Yes, but if a stranger got in, and was drunk and loud, unsteady on his feet, she may have been spooked. You couldn't blame the animal," Weldon said.

"Well, let's wait and see, shall we? The Gardaí have a team on the way. And for God's sake don't say anything to Jenny. She's not stupid. If Lady did kick him to death, she knows what the consequences will be, and that would destroy her."

It seemed no time at all before four Garda vehicles arrived in quick succession from Galway. In the lead was Sally Fahy in her white Hyundai squad car. She had the good sense to turn off the sirens as she approached the show ground so as not to frighten any of the ponies who had started to go through their routines out in the arena.

Next to arrive was Sinéad Loughran in her unmarked Toyota Land Cruiser, favoured by the forensic team for its off-road capabilities. Sinéad had two more forensic technicians with her, and as soon as they had parked the jeep and got out, all three donned white paper suits and blue vinyl gloves before approaching the taped off horsebox. Sinéad gave one of the uniformed Gardaí a clipboard, instructing him to record anyone who went inside the cordon so that fingerprints and shoe prints could be eliminated if the need arose.

Lyons and Flynn arrived next. As soon as they had got into the car in Galway, Lyons had called Dr Julian Dodd, the pathologist; Sinéad, the forensic team lead; and Superintendent Finbarr Plunkett on her mobile phone.

Dodd was last to arrive in his almost new Lexus. Although he was an excellent pathologist, his manner often left something to be desired. The detectives put this down to his diminutive stature, but on this occasion, he appeared to be quite subdued. He was, as always, dapper, sporting a green and brown tweed suit and stout all-leather brogues.

"Good morning, Inspector. This long drive out through Connemara is becoming somewhat of a habit, don't you think? What have you managed to dig up for me today?" he said.

"This looks pretty straightforward, Doc. A man was found in the back of this horsebox with what looks like a head injury. They're saying he may have got in when he was a bit the worse for wear, and the pony got spooked and kicked him in the head," Lyons said.

"And the people who are saying this are, no doubt, trained pathologists?"

"Well no, of course not. That's why we sent for you, Doctor," she said.

"Very well. I'll get started. Who's that inside the cordon?" Dodd asked.

"That's the father of the girl that owns the pony," Lyons said.

"Well get him out of there will you, for heaven's sake? Oh, and by the way, where is the animal?" Dodd asked.

"She's been put into one of the stables with her owner."

* * *

As the show started to get busy, other owners and competitors, on hearing the story, stopped by the stable where Jenny, her mother and Lady were resting. It didn't take long for the rumour that Lady had in all probability kicked the man to death to filter into the stable, and one particularly insensitive man blurted out, "Of course, you do realize the animal will have to be put down now," in a loud voice so that it could be heard inside.

On hearing this prediction, Jenny lost it. Her brain went into melt-down at the thought of losing her beloved horse and best friend, and it all became too much for her to bear. She ran out of the stable, pushing past the man, nearly knocking him over, and ran sobbing out of the show grounds. She ran and ran. Off down through the town, and out across the fields, on and on until she felt her lungs would burst. By the time she came to a stop, totally out of breath, she had no idea where she was and couldn't care less. Máiréad, the girl's mother, didn't know whether to chase after her or to stay with Lady, who had become restive again in response Jenny's antics. She decided to stay put and try to placate the pony, giving the man a stern look. He took the hint, and wandered off without another word.

Chapter Four

When the doctor had been working for a few minutes kneeling down beside the prone corpse of the dead man, he called out to Lyons.

"Inspector, over here please, if you will."

Lyons lifted the tape and ducked under.

"Two things, Inspector. Firstly, this man was not killed by an animal. In fact, he wasn't kicked by the pony at all. He has, as you observed, a head injury, but it was quite definitely not inflicted by a horse's hoof, and in any case, it wasn't of sufficient ferocity to kill him," the doctor said.

"How do you know, Doctor?" Lyons said.

"Dear lady, I have been doing this job for almost thirty years, and I have seen many an unfortunate soul whose life was extinguished by the rear leg of a horse, and I can say categorically that this is not one of those injuries. A shod horse leaves a very distinctive arc shaped indentation at the site of the injury. This man's wound is linear – quite impossible for an animal to inflict. Furthermore, the blow to the head is not what killed him.

It's quite superficial. Enough for him to need a few paracetamol tablets, and he probably would have blacked out for a few minutes, but that's it," said the doctor finishing his speech.

"I see. And the second thing?" Lyons said.

"He wasn't killed here. He was killed elsewhere and then placed in the horsebox, presumably so that folks would think that the wretched pony had seen him off. Seems to have worked too, from what I hear."

Dr Dodd then held up his hand to prevent Lyons from speaking.

"I know, Inspector. What did he die of? When did he die? Who killed him, and why? Frankly, I haven't a clue, but I'll know more when I get him back to Galway and look inside. But I can say that he probably did bleed a bit wherever he was struck, and I'd say he died about twelve hours ago, give or take, so sometime between eight and ten last night," he said.

"OK, thanks, Doc. So we have a murder on our hands – again. Can I just go through his pockets before you cart him off? I'd like to identify him if possible," Lyons said.

"Yes, of course. Help yourself," the doctor said gesturing towards the body.

"Shall we say ten o'clock tomorrow morning?" Dodd said.

"Yes, OK, fine. See you then."

The doctor packed the implements of his trade away in his old leather bag and left the scene, wiping his shoes on the grass at the edge of the path before getting back into his car. When Lyons had finished fishing in the dead man's pockets, the body was placed in a strong plastic zip-up bag and then taken away in an anonymous black Mercedes van to the mortuary in Galway where the post mortem would be performed.

Lyons removed herself from the back of the horsebox and found Sally Fahy standing nearby.

"Sally can you find out who's in charge here? See if they can give us an office or somewhere we can set up an incident room. We could use the Garda station, but it would be better to be on site if possible," Lyons said.

"Sure. I'll call you when I have something organised," Fahy said, heading off towards the show office.

Then Lyons went and found Eamon Flynn. She knew they had no time to lose in getting the investigation underway.

"Eamon. Can you go and find the pony that was in the box? Sinéad will probably need to examine its hooves, and make sure they don't clean it up, there may be hair or blood or other evidence caught in one of its shoes," Lyons said.

"And when you've done that, start setting up interviews with anyone who stayed overnight at the show ground. There are a number of camper vans lined up along the far side of the car park, and some of the bigger horse trailers also have quite luxurious living accommodation built into them. Get one of the uniforms to help you. This lot will want to be leaving soon, and we need to talk to them before they disappear. You should be able to get a list from the office," Lyons said.

"What about the girl?" Flynn asked.

"She'll probably turn up in an hour or two. We've enough to be doing for now," she said.

Lyons then walked back to Lady's trailer where Sinéad was finishing up.

"Sinéad, I need you and your crew to have a good look around for wherever this fella was set upon. The doc says he wasn't killed in the horsebox, so we need to find where the initial attack took place. There could be some blood evidence where he was hit on the head. Give the place a good going over for us. Did you find anything in the horsebox?" she said.

"A good few prints on the back door, around the hasps, as you'd expect. A couple of boot prints on the floor underneath the straw, oh and some horse poo!"

"Lovely. Good for the roses though," Lyons said, smirking. "Give me a call if you find anything," she said, walking away towards the office.

* * *

The show office looked like organised chaos when Lyons arrived. It was a permanent structure with wooden steps up to a half-glazed green door, with the word "Office" painted in signwriting on cream coloured board over the entrance. Inside, there were three desks, each one piled high with papers and folders, leaving just a small space for the three girls occupying the office to work. There were wooden bookshelves all around three of the walls to waist height, leaving a shelf on top which was festooned with trophies of all shapes and sizes. The centrepiece was a large silver cup sitting on a black wooden base, and Lyons could just make out "Best in Show" engraved along the side of it.

Above the shelving were numerous photographs, mostly black and white, of ponies with their proud owners, and some of these included behatted dignitaries with chains of office presenting cups or rosettes. Many of the photos had captions along the lines of "Moygashel – winner 1972" and so on.

The fourth wall of the crowded office had another half-glazed door leading to a small office with "Show Manager" printed on white card and pinned to it with a brass drawing pin. Through the glass Lyons could see Sally Fahy trying to clear some space on the manager's desk and arranging the room so that a briefing could be held.

Lyons asked the girl sitting at the desk nearest the entrance, "Where can I find Mr Weldon?"

"He'll be back in a minute. He's just gone down to see the Gillespies. God, this is awful," she said.

"Can you get him on the radio or send someone to fetch him. I need to talk to him urgently," Lyons said.

"Yes, OK. I'll go myself. I won't be long," she said getting up and putting on a sleeveless padded green jacket.

Weldon appeared back in the office a few minutes later.

"Hello, Inspector, I hear you want to see me," he said.

Oliver Weldon was a man in his fifties who spoke with a refined Galway accent. He was a stocky man of about five feet nine in height with a generous mop of silver hair and a ruddy face. He was wearing the by now familiar green padded sleeveless jacket over a grey button-down Ralph Lauren shirt and somewhat worn dark green corduroy trousers that topped a pair of stout brown leather brogues.

"Thank you, Mr Weldon. Yes, I just wanted to update you and your team with some news we have from the pathologist, Dr Dodd," Lyons said.

"The good doctor has confirmed that the dead man was not killed by the pony, in fact the animal never touched him. The man was dead before he entered the horsebox. He was killed elsewhere," Lyons said. Weldon went to speak, but Lyons carried on before he got a chance to get going.

"We now have a murder investigation underway, Mr Weldon, so we need to treat the whole area around the pony's trailer as a crime scene, and we need to interview anyone who was here late last night, or overnight," she said.

"I see. Well, yes, of course. Would it be OK to let the Gillespies know that Lady is in the clear? Jenny is very upset."

"Yes, that's not a problem, it could even help us," Lyons said.

Weldon despatched one of the girls to go to the stable where Lady was temporarily housed to break the good news. As she left, Lyons' phone started to ring and she excused herself, going outside to take the call from Sinéad Loughran, the forensic team lead.

"Yes Sinéad, what's up?"

"Hi Maureen. We've found a small patch of blood on the ground at the back of the stable block. And there are some scuff marks on the ground here too. I can't say for sure if it's the victim's blood, but the chances are," Sinéad said.

"OK. Well you know what to do. I'll come down in a few minutes, I just want to sort out a few things up at the office," Lyons said.

Lyons went back in to where Sally Fahy was re-arranging Weldon's office. She had cleared enough space for five chairs, and had managed to procure a blackboard from somewhere that she had propped up against the wall behind Weldon's desk.

"That's great Sally, well done," Lyons said, and went on to tell the junior detective what had been discovered.

"We'll have a briefing in an hour here. Tell the rest of them for me, will you?"

Just then a commotion broke out in the main office. Máiréad Gillespie had come back as soon as she heard that Lady had been cleared, and she was now calling for the Gardaí to find her daughter.

Lyons nodded to Fahy, who took the hint and went out into the general office to deal with the distraught woman.

"You must find Jenny. She has to know that Lady isn't going to be put down," Máiréad Gillespie said between sobs. "She's very upset, and anything could have happened to her."

"It's all right, Mrs Gillespie," Fahy re-assured the woman, "We'll find her. She won't have gone far. I'll get someone onto it at once. Now why don't you go back to the stables? That's where Jenny will go when she comes back."

When Mrs Gillespie had left the office somewhat reluctantly, Lyons spoke to Fahy again.

"Sally, you'd better get on to Séan Mulholland. Ask him to take any spare uniformed officers he can find and start a search for the girl. Get him to comb out the town, you know, the coffee shops, pubs, and ask about. She can't be far away, and if they find her, be sure to tell her the pony is safe. This is all we bloody need!"

When things had quietened down a little, and she had set a number of investigative strands running, Lyons turned her attention to the dead man. She had retrieved his wallet and car keys from his pocket before the doctor had arranged for the body to be taken away, and, wearing vinyl gloves so as not to contaminate the evidence, she laid the contents of the wallet out on the desk in Weldon's office.

There were five plastic cards in the wallet. A UK driver's license with a photo of the man taken a few years back by the look of it, an Irish passport card valid for a further four years, an AIB bank card in his own name, and an HSBC debit card as well as a Barclaycard, all in date, and all correct as far as Lyons could see.

Further exploration of the brown leather wallet revealed €350 in cash, a number of receipts for petrol and food in Galway, an out-of-date membership card for an organisation called "The Association of Journalistic Photographers" and a recent receipt from a place called Ocean View Guesthouse, handwritten, and signed in a fluid hand by what looked like C Curley.

Lyons put the items into a plastic evidence bag and sealed it tightly. Then she left the office and went to the back of the stable block where Sinéad Loughran was sifting around. Along the back wall of several concrete stables a number of large plastic bins with sliding lids were lined up. The bins were in different colours signifying the way in which garbage had to be sorted for disposal and recycling. Sinéad was working at the side of one of the bins, dusting the ground with a narrow paint brush. She still had her hooded white paper suit on, and her face was covered with a white face mask to prevent her inhaling any of the dust that was being thrown up.

When Lyons appeared, Sinéad stood up and removed her mask and hood, allowing her blonde ponytail to fall loosely down her back.

The two women knew each other well, and unless there was an audience, they tended to dispense with the usual formalities.

"Hi Maureen," the forensic girl said, "I think this may be where the victim was attacked. There's a fairly small blood spill, and there are some hand smudges on the lid and side of the green bin where he may have reached out as he fell to the ground."

"Any sign of a weapon?" Lyons said.

"Not yet, but when I've finished I'll have one of the guys go through the bins," Sinéad said.

"Lucky him! How much longer will you be?"

"No more than an hour. I'll come and find you when we're done," Sinéad said.

* * *

Sergeant Séan Mulholland was quite enjoying the drama of the missing girl. It wasn't often that something like this came along to punctuate the otherwise drab daily grind, and he felt that the girl wasn't in any real danger in any case. But they needed to find her, if for no other reason than to put her mind at rest about her pony.

He had commandeered two of the uniformed Gardaí that had been allocated to the show, and along with two more of his own uniformed officers, they had set out through Clifden to make enquiries. They had divided the town and its hinterland up into rectangles, and they went from premises to premises looking for Jenny Gillespie. They didn't have a photograph of her, but they reckoned that a dark-haired fifteen-year-old girl with a Donegal accent wearing riding gear wouldn't be too hard to spot.

At the same time, two more of Mulholland's men, Jim Dolan and Peadar Toner, set off in two separate cars to drive out along the roads leading from the town in case she had gone further afield. But despite all of their enquiries and searching, there was no sign of the girl by lunchtime when they all met up at Clifden's Garda station to compare notes.

Chapter Five

Lyons got the team together just after lunch. They were all packed into Oliver Weldon's office, seated rather uncomfortably on chairs that Sally had borrowed from the general office outside. There were just five names chalked up on the blackboard. At the top was David Ellis, the deceased. Beneath the victim's name was Jenny Gillespie – missing, followed by the names of her mother and father. At the end of the list was the single word – Lady.

"OK," Lyons said, "what have we got. Sinéad?"

Sinéad Loughran explained how the body had been found positioned to make it look as if the pony had kicked the victim to death. She went on to explain that this was not the case. She explained about the site they had found by the bins, and revealed that on going through them, right at the bottom of the blue bin, they had found a hypodermic syringe. At first she had thought that it could have been used for one of the animals, but Sinéad had consulted the on-site vet and she had confirmed that it was not of the kind used on horses. There was a small trace of clear liquid left in the syringe, but Sinéad had not had a chance to determine what it was.

"But that doesn't mean it has anything to do with Ellis's death, surely?" said Eamon Flynn.

"I agree. But it's a bit odd. Anyone injecting themselves for diabetes, say, wouldn't discard a syringe with the needle still attached like that," Sinéad said.

"Oh, and we found a stout piece of wood about a foot long discarded in one of the other bins. It may be what was used to bash Ellis over the head. I'll have to get it back into the lab to be sure – see if there are any blood traces or hair on it. I'm sorry, but there won't be any fingerprints on it," she continued.

"OK. Let's move on. Eamon how have the interviews gone?" Lyons said.

"We set up three separate streams and focused on the people who had stayed overnight here on the grounds. No one saw anything out of the ordinary. No one suspicious lurking around, and everyone we spoke to seemed to have someone else who could vouch for them. So, more or less a complete blank. Sorry, boss," he said.

"Great. Sally did any of the staff have anything useful to add?"

"No, nothing I'm afraid. But I did sense that something wasn't quite right as I was talking to them. Nothing you could put your finger on – just a feeling really – you know, the occasional furtive look between them, poor eye contact sometimes, that sort of thing," the young detective said.

"Hmm, OK, that's interesting. We'll follow up on that later. Well spotted, Sally. What about the security company that are supposed to guard the place after hours?" Lyons said.

"Nothing there either, boss. It seems they only do a drive by every two hours or so, and there was nothing reported, so that's a dead end too," Flynn said.

"Terrific! Right, well here are our tasks for the rest of the day. Eamon, can you locate this Ocean View place and see what you can find out? If he was staying there, drive out and go through his room, see what you can turn up. Sally, can you get on to John O'Connor. Give him the details of the license, passport and cards and see what he can dig up on our Mr Ellis? Sinéad, can you come with me? I want to see if we can find Ellis's car, and then I have to call Superintendent Plunkett and put him in the picture," Lyons said. "Let's meet back at six for an update."

* * *

Cathleen Curley had completed all of her household chores and had finished a late lunch with her husband when Eamon Flynn turned into the drive and parked in front of Ocean View.

When he had introduced himself to the woman of the house, he confirmed that she had a Mr David Ellis staying.

"Yes, Mr Ellis is a nice man, but very quiet you know. He doesn't say much," she said.

"How many nights is he booked in for, Mrs Curley?" Flynn asked.

"Well he should by rights have checked out today, but, well, he didn't actually come back here at all last night. He might have met someone you know, that sometimes happens. And it's no harm, his room isn't booked for tonight what with the show being over. It'll be quiet enough now till the Arts Festival next month," Mrs Curley said.

Flynn asked the woman to sit down and informed her that they had found the body of a man they believed to be David Ellis at the pony show grounds. She was, of course, distraught. So much so that Flynn insisted on making her a strong cup of sugary tea. He then asked if he could examine the room that Ellis had been staying in, and Cathleen readily agreed.

Flynn found the room to be very neat and tidy. There was just one extra pair of trousers hanging in the wardrobe, a freshly pressed shirt, two pairs of socks and a clean pair of underpants in the drawers. A small black alarm clock ticked quietly on the night stand beside the bed where a half-finished tumbler of water also stood. A small black carry-on bag was placed on the only chair in the room. The small ensuite shower room yielded the usual toiletries that accompany a single man travelling alone, and a plastic supermarket bag with some used socks and undies lay in the corner of the room against the wall.

Flynn explored the room carefully, looking underneath the clothes in the drawer, and examining the pockets of the trousers, but found nothing of interest. He was about to leave the room when he had an idea. Rather reluctantly, for he disliked disturbing the neat, well-made bed, he lifted the mattress. It was heavy, and to see underneath it properly he had to sit on the base of the double bed and perch the mattress on his shoulder whilst he felt around in the gap. But his efforts were well rewarded. There, tucked in snugly between the mattress and the base of the bed, he found a small, slim laptop computer.

After he had donned blue plastic gloves, he repeated the acrobatics with the mattress and fished out the little computer which he recognised as a small Apple MacBook. When he had re-assembled the bed in a sort of fashion, he sat on the edge and phoned Lyons.

"That's great, well done, Eamon. Don't touch it or turn it on. Take it in to John O'Connor and get him going on it first thing tomorrow."

* * *

Using the car keys Lyons had retrieved from Ellis's jacket pocket, Sinéad and Lyons moved amongst the remaining cars parked in the show ground with Lyons continually pressing the remote fob that would open car doors and probably flash the lights too. By the time they had circled the car park twice, none of the vehicles had responded.

Lyons handed the keys to Sinéad.

"Can you go out on the road and try these on the cars parked up and down the street outside? I want to call Dr Dodd to see if he's got anything further," Lyons said.

Sinéad Loughran left the show grounds, making an odd sight in the street outside still dressed in her scene of crime suit, although she had at least removed her face mask.

* * *

"Ah, Inspector, I was wondering if you would call. I think I may have discovered what killed your Mr Ellis," Dodd said.

"Excellent, Doctor. Go on then, what was it?" Lyons said.

"I'd say it was almost certainly cyanide. The poor man smelled so strongly of almonds I thought someone had opened a packet of Amaretti biscuits here in the mortuary. I didn't detect it out at the scene, the smell was covered up by horse droppings and urine, but once we got him back here, it was unmistakeable. There's enough of it in him to kill a horse, if you'll pardon the pun," the doctor said.

"I see. And have you any idea how it might have been administered, Doctor?"

"Yes, I have, Inspector. There was a small puncture mark and a little post mortem bruising starting to appear on his neck. If I were you I'd start looking around for a fine pointed needle attached to a hypodermic syringe," he said.

"Already done, Doctor. We found it in a rubbish bin at the back of the stables. We just didn't know what it contained," Lyons said.

"Well I should handle it very carefully, Inspector. That stuff can be lethal, as your victim discovered to his cost."

"Just one more thing, Doctor. How easy is it to get hold of a lethal dose of cyanide these days?" Lyons said.

"All too easy, Inspector. You can even distil it from rock or metal if you know how. But it's more commonly found in insecticides, or rat poison, or in commercial processing of batteries or printed circuits," Dodd said.

"And how much would you need to kill someone?"

"That's two more things, Inspector. About 300 milligrams would do it, or much less if it was in concentrated form as I'm sure I'll find this is."

"Thanks, Doc. I'll see you tomorrow for the full PM," Lyons said.

Chapter Six

Jenny Gillespie found herself down by the edge of the sea, sitting on some rocks. The sky had clouded over quite a bit, and there was a cool breeze beginning to blow in off the water. Further out, above the vast expanse of the Atlantic Ocean, thick grey clouds, laden with rain, were approaching.

Jenny had calmed down quite a bit, and had been processing the events of earlier in the day thoroughly. She wasn't a stupid girl, and she felt sure now that even if Lady had killed that man, it would be unlikely that the animal would be slaughtered for it. She knew that dogs that had turned vicious were often put down after they had bitten someone, but this was different, and besides, her parents would do all that they could to protect the pony. Maybe she had over-reacted, she thought.

She didn't have a watch, nor had she the presence of mind to bring her phone when she ran off from the show grounds, but she knew instinctively that it must be well into the afternoon. She should go back – but how? She was lost.

As she sat there trying to figure out which way to set off to get her back to the show, a dark green Land Rover with a single occupant came along bouncing over the rough ground to where she was sitting. The vehicle was driven by a man who looked to be in his early forties with sandy coloured hair and a kind face.

"Hello there," he said through the open window, bringing the jeep to a halt with a squeal of brakes.

"Hi," she replied, a little unsure if she should engage with this stranger.

"Are you OK? You look frozen," the man said.

"No, I'm fine thanks. Listen, you couldn't direct me back to the pony show, could you?" Jenny said.

"Yeah, sure. Better than that, I'll give you a lift. Hop in!" he said beckoning her to the passenger side of the car.

Jenny didn't immediately climb into the Land Rover. The driver, sensing her reluctance, said, "It's OK. You're quite safe. I'm a teacher in the local school. I have lots of pupils your age."

Jenny was re-assured by this, and he had a nice smile, in fact he was quite attractive, so she walked around in front of the jeep and climbed in.

"Hi. I'm Tony Halpin. What's your name?" the teacher said.

"Jenny, Jenny Gillespie," she said putting out her hand and shaking his.

Halpin turned the Land Rover around and headed back along the rough, rocky track. As he navigated the bumpy ground, he said, "I'll have you back at the show grounds in a few minutes, but do you mind if we stop at my place for two secs on the way, I have some things to collect?"

Jenny wasn't too happy with this new development, and looked quite nervous.

"It's OK. You can stay in the car if you like. I'll only be a moment or two," Halpin said.

She realised she was being silly. After all he had been kind enough to stop and offer her a lift; and anyway, he was quite hunky, she thought to herself.

"Sorry, yes of course, no problem," Jenny said.

Halpin drove the two of them to the outskirts of Clifden and then turned down another narrow track that led to a modest bungalow standing on a patch of rough gravel. The house appeared to be in quite poor condition, though there would be fantastic views from the back of the property out across Clifden Bay.

As Halpin brought the Land Rover to a halt, he said to Jenny, "Look, why don't you come in for a minute while I get my things. You can make a cup of tea, and I think I even have a few chocolate biscuits."

Jenny hadn't realised just how hungry she had become, and the thought of a warming cuppa and a few biscuits allowed her to overcome her naturally cautious instincts.

"You know, you really are a very pretty girl. I love your hair," he said as he opened the front door and stood to the side to let her brush past him into the bungalow.

The house was no tidier inside than the outside had indicated. In the kitchen, the sink was crammed with dirty dishes, and some very dirty tea-towels were scattered around. Jenny filled the kettle, and lit the small gas stove with a match she took from a box she found on the kitchen table, and in a few minutes the kettle was singing nicely. She found a packet of teabags on a shelf over the sink, and rinsed out a cup as best she could, before pouring the boiling water into it on top of the teabag. There was no sign of any of the promised chocolate biscuits, and there didn't appear to be a fridge, or any milk either.

Halpin was rooting around in the other room, and came back into the kitchen a minute later.

"OK. I've got my things now. Are you ready to go?" he said.

"Yeah, I didn't get any tea or biscuits though – there's no milk. This place is a tip," she said sourly.

"Well, never mind. We'll get you something when we get back into town," he said, heading for the front door.

Chapter Seven

As Lyons was making her way back to Weldon's office, her mobile phone rang.

"Inspector, it's Superintendent Plunkett. How are things going out there?" he said.

"Good afternoon, sir. Well, we now know who the dead man is, a Mr David Ellis. It looks like he was given a lethal injection of cyanide after he was rendered unconscious with a bash on the head. So far that's about all we've got – oh, and the girl who owns the pony in the horsebox where the body was found has gone missing, sir," Lyons said.

"Jesus. Sounds like a bit of a muddle, Inspector. Do you need more men?"

"Well it's early days, sir, and we have the four extra Gardaí who were posted out here for the show, so I think we're OK for now," she said.

"Right. Well you should know that I've had a call from Oliver Weldon. His wife plays bridge with Mrs Plunkett. He's not too happy. He says the publicity will be very damaging for the show and he wants his office back too. See if you can calm him down a bit, will you? He's an important figure in the community out in Clifden you know. And keep me updated, won't you?"

"Yes, sir, will do, of course, sir."

Lyons had just arrived back in Weldon's office and was sitting at his desk taking a minute to collect her thoughts when a row broke out in the general office outside the manager's door.

Mrs Máiréad Gillespie had come crashing into the room.

"Who's in charge here? I want to speak to him, now!" she shrieked.

Lyons beckoned through the glass door for the woman to come in.

"Who are you?" demanded Mrs Gillespie as she swept into the inner office. "Where's the officer in charge?"

"I'm Inspector Lyons, and I'm the officer in charge. May I ask who you are?" Lyons said, although she knew full well that it was the mother of the girl who owned the pony.

"Máiréad Gillespie," she snapped, "my daughter is missing and you lot don't seem to be doing anything about it."

"Please sit down, Mrs Gillespie. Would you like a glass of water, or a cup of tea?" Lyons asked.

"No, I would not. I'd like my daughter back," she said, now a little tearful as she plonked herself down on the sparc chair.

"Yes, of course. Let me explain what we are actually doing to find Jenny." Lyons went on to outline the search that Séan Mulholland had organised.

"She really can't be very far, Mrs Gillespie, I'm sure she'll turn up shortly. It must have been very distressing for her, but she'll be fine," Lyons said.

"Well I hope you're right. If any harm comes to her, I'll hold you personally responsible. I'm not without influence you know."

When the woman had calmed down and left the office, Lyons put a call in to the station and spoke to Sergeant Mulholland.

"Hi, Séan. I've just had the Gillespie woman in giving me a right earful about her daughter, as if there wasn't enough going on without having to deal with truculent teenagers and their mothers. Any news?"

"Hi Maureen. Well I have a good team out searching now. There were one or two reports of a possible sighting. A couple of the locals said they thought they saw a teenage girl travelling in the passenger seat of a Land Rover near the town," Mulholland said.

"Oh well, that's good. Do we know who the jeep belongs to?"

"That's just it. It may not be such good news. We think it might be Tony Halpin's vehicle. We know Halpin. He was a teacher out at the secondary school last year, doing physical education, games, that sort of thing," Mulholland said.

"And?"

"Well the school had to let him go. Some complaints were received from the parents that he'd been a bit too 'hands-on' with some of the girls. There was never enough hard evidence to do anything about it, but all the same," Mulholland said.

"Jesus, Séan, so you're telling me that Jenny has fallen into the hands of the local pedo. For fuck's sake!"

"Ah now, steady up Maureen. I have a few of the lads on their way out to his place now. She'll not come to any harm, don't fret. We'll have her back in no time," Mulholland said, but Lyons wasn't convinced.

* * *

As Lyons sat in the cramped little office on her own, she tried to take stock of the situation. She wished she had Mick Hays by her side to guide her a bit and provide some cover. She knew she was a little out of her depth, but she also knew that she couldn't afford to show any signs of uncertainty or indecision in front of her team.

"Damn it girl, get a grip," she said to herself. She decided that as there was little she could do for the dead man at this stage, they should concentrate on getting the girl back safely for now.

Outside, the show ground was thinning out. Most of the competitors had left, keen to get themselves and their animals away from the morbid scene. All of their details had been recorded, so there was no need to detain them.

Lyons found Sally Fahy coming back in from the road outside the venue.

"Hi Sally, anything new?" Lyons said.

"Not really, no. Sinéad is just finishing up with Ellis's car, but there's nothing much there, though he has had a passenger in it recently – there's still some slightly damp mud in the footwell on the passenger's side. Not enough for a shoe print though," Fahy said.

"OK, well you and I are going to see if we can locate Jenny Gillespie. She has to be somewhere close by. Mulholland sent his men out to the house owned by the driver of the car she was seen in, but there's no one there. Let's you and I use our very best powers of detection to figure out where he's taken her. Can you bring your car around?" Lyons said.

The two detectives drove to the Abbey Glen Hotel where the Gillespies were staying for the duration of the show. When they went inside, they found a tall young man with a pimply complexion moving cases around the expansive foyer.

Lyons walked over to him and introduced herself.

"And may I have your name?" she asked.

"Peter. Peter Dowdall," the lad replied.

"I'm Inspector Maureen Lyons. We are trying to find Jenny Gillespie. She's staying here with her parents. Have you seen her at all today, Peter?"

"Well, I saw them this morning. They left for the show just after breakfast," the lad said.

Lyons guessed that the boy was about sixteen or seventeen years old, so she took a chance and asked him, "Sorry, can I ask you, do you go to the local secondary school here in Clifden?"

"Yes, I do as it happens. I'm in the sixth year. I've just got this job here for the summer. It's dead handy."

"Great. Do you know a Mr Tony Halpin?" Lyons asked.

"That prick. Yeah, I know him."

"You don't have a lot of time for him then? Why is that?"

"He's a weirdo, that's why. He tries it on with all the senior girls. He even tried it on with a girl I was going out with. He took her out in that jeep of his and tried to kiss her, bloody pedo."

"Really. Where did he take her, your girlfriend I mean?"

"Out by the island where they do the point to point racing, Omey I think it's called," Peter said.

"Thanks, Peter. C'mon Sally, let's go!"

Lyons sat in beside Sally Fahy in her smart little Ford Focus and took out the map.

"Let's see. Halpin's house is here, out on the Skye Road," she said pointing to a spot on the map, "it's just after the start of the loop." Lyons mused.

"Look, there," Fahy said, pointing to Omey Island, out near Claddaghduff. "That's where they do the pony races in the summer. And you can drive across to the island at low tide – especially in a Land Rover!"

"Great! Let's get out there as quick as we can."

* * *

"What are we doing here?" Jenny Gillespie said to Halpin as he brought the old Land Rover to a halt on the clear white sand of Omey Beach. The view looking out to the island in the distance was truly spectacular. The sun was getting lower now, and it made the sea look like a huge wrinkly mirror as wisps of thin fluffy clouds in the sky above were reflected on the sea's surface.

"I just thought you'd like to see where they have the point to point races. It's great fun," Halpin said.

"Well, yes, thanks. But I really need to get back now. My parents will be worried, and I want to see my pony," Jenny said.

"In a minute," Halpin said, sliding across the bench seat in the old jeep in Jenny's direction. He put his left hand on her left shoulder and tried to draw her close.

"What are you doing? Stop!" she said.

"Just one kiss, Jenny, then we'll go," he said, moving in even closer.

"No, no! Stop it! Let me out," she shouted, pushing herself up against the passenger's door. Jenny fumbled for the door handle to open it and escape, but when she found it, it wouldn't budge.

"Come here you little tease. You know you want it," Halpin said. A cold, cruel tone had come into his voice, and his eyes had flared. He put his right hand down firmly on the girl's jeans, high up on her inner thigh.

Jenny screamed.

As Tony Halpin moved closer, he spotted Fahy's car approaching in the Land Rover's wing mirror.

"Oh, shit!" he said as he quickly scrambled back over into the driver's seat and started the jeep. He took off across the causeway leading to the island. The tide was starting to come in, and as he gathered speed the old jeep threw up a solid sheet of sea spray. Sally Fahy pursued the Land Rover which was now just a dark hulk in her windscreen awash with salty sea water, smearing the window with a white scum, obscuring her vision.

When Jenny saw what was happening she was sure that the car behind contained her rescuers. As the jeep sped up, she leaned across and grabbed the steering wheel, wresting it free from Halpin's grip, and heaved hard on it. The old jeep went up on two wheels momentarily, left the track and plunged up to its waist into a deep pool off to the side of the makeshift track. With an enormous splash, it came to rest, its engine slowly drowning in the deep salt water.

By the time Halpin had gathered his thoughts, Lyons was opening the driver's door, warrant card in hand.

"Tony Halpin, I'm arresting you on suspicion of abduction of a minor." She continued reading out the rest of his rights. Fahy in the meantime had managed to open the passenger's door and was comforting Jenny who was sobbing loudly, more from relief than anything else.

The soggy quartet made their way back to Clifden's Garda station in Fahy's Focus which had remained high and relatively dry on the causeway leading out to the island.

"What are you going to do about my Land Rover?" Halpin asked as they drove along.

"I shouldn't worry about it, Mr Halpin. By the time you get processed in Clifden I reckon the tide will have taken care of your car for you, don't you?" Lyons said, smiling.

Before they reached the town, Sally had re-assured Jenny Gillespie that her beloved pony was alive and well, and had been found not guilty of killing David Ellis. Fahy had let her call her mother on her phone too, and Máiréad arranged to meet them at the Garda station. Máiréad would accompany her daughter, who was only too willing to make a statement against the amorous teacher.

When Mulholland saw the entourage coming in to the station, he couldn't believe his eyes.

"Good God! You lot look as if you have all been swimming in your clothes," he exclaimed.

"Yes, Séan," Lyons said, "and just look at the nasty little sea monster we caught too."

"Ah, yes, Mr Halpin. We've met before, haven't we?" Mulholland said.

Halpin gave the sergeant a dirty look.

Halpin was booked in, and Jenny's mother arrived a few minutes later. When mother and daughter had been tearfully re-united, Jenny gave her account to the sergeant, and the two of them were allowed to go back to see Lady and get on their way home. The Gillespies wouldn't forget this pony show in a hurry.

Chapter Eight

Back at the show ground things were coming to a close as the evening drew in. The fences in the arena had been dismantled, and an army of cleaners were going around emptying bins, and clearing up papers and discarded food wrappers. In two days' time the show ground would be hosting the Galway Vintage Classic Car and Bike Show, so there was no time to waste getting the place ready.

Oliver Weldon had taken back possession of his office and was just finishing putting all his stuff back in its rightful place when Lyons and Fahy arrived.

"Well, Mr Weldon, you'll be pleased to get the place back to normal," Lyons said.

"I'm not sure it will ever feel the same again to be honest. I can't get the image of that poor man lying dead in the horsebox out of my mind," he said.

"It will pass, given time, Mr Weldon, trust me. Thanks for the use of the office and your co-operation. We'll be moving all this stuff back to Galway tonight, but we will need to talk to you again at some stage," Lyons said.

"That's fine. I'll be around for the next few weeks. It's quite a busy time for us after the show. I'll get away to the Canaries for a break after Christmas," he said.

Lyons asked Sally Fahy to make sure all the paperwork was properly boxed up and said she was off home. She asked the younger detective to arrange a briefing for 9 a.m. the following morning in Mill Street.

As Lyons drove back along the N59 towards the city, she was once again taken by the sheer beauty of her surroundings. Late summer was the best time of year for Connemara, she thought, while there was still some modest growth in the hedgerows, and the heathers had come into full bloom. Here and there in the more sheltered parts, wild fuchsia bushes pushed out their bright red, pink and purple trumpet-like blooms, giving the bees a last chance to stock up on nectar before the grey, misty days of winter descended on the countryside. The evening sun was setting gently out to sea, casting long shadows from the distant Twelve Pins on the boggy terrain.

* * *

It was after ten o'clock when Lyons got back to the house she shared with Mick Hays in Salthill. Hays had telephoned her from his hotel in the UK as she drove home, but she only spent a moment talking to him, promising to call him back when she got indoors. When she had changed out of her still damp work clothes into pyjamas – garments rarely used when Mick was at home – and scoffed down some re-heated lasagne from the fridge, she made the call.

She filled him in on the events of the day.

"Cripes Maureen, sounds like you're up to your neck in it. I'm sorry I'm not there for you. If you like I can cut this short and come home," Hays said when he heard about the goings on out in Clifden.

"Not at all, you're grand. We'll get on top of this tomorrow when I get the team together. It's about time I learned to stand on my own two feet anyway," she said, not meaning a word of it. She missed him terribly. Not just for the support he always gave freely in the job, but at a personal level as well. She had spent too many lonely nights before they got together, and she was longing to feel him close beside her as they drifted off to sleep.

"Well this thing finishes up tomorrow just after lunch, and I was planning on doing some sight-seeing in the afternoon. My flight back is the day after at three o'clock. It was the cheapest one on the Ryanair web site," he said.

"That's fine. You stick to your plan and we'll have this nonsense all sewn up by the time you get back, you'll see. How's the course going anyway?" Lyons said.

"It was much better today, thank heavens. We got onto some quite advanced stuff about setting up traces on the web, and using mobile phone data that the user doesn't even know is there, to track people. I bet you didn't know that every mobile phone in the world is capable of being listened into by the authorities," Hays said.

"No, I didn't. Scary stuff," she said.

"And I've met a nice DCI from the local force here. His name is Richard Gibson. He's going to take me to one of his favourite inns in about half an hour for a few pints and a nice meal. There are some really lovely English pubs in this area," Hays said.

"Cool. You'll enjoy that," she said, "But Mick."

"Yeah?"

"I'm missing you like crazy, ye big eejit."

"Nice. But I know what you mean. Me too – lots."

They said goodnight.

* * *

When Lyons arrived at Mill Street the next morning she brought the team together.

"Right, listen up everybody, we've got a busy day ahead," she said, standing in front of the whiteboard where a photograph of David Ellis had been pinned up.

"By the end of the day, I want to know everything there is to know about David Ellis. John, will you get busy with his laptop? It's probably password protected, but I'm sure you can get past that easily enough. Search everything that's on there, and when you need a break from that, look at his Facebook, Snapchat, LinkedIn and any other social media connections you can find. Anything significant, bring it to me at once, don't wait till the end of the day," Lyons said.

John O'Connor relished the challenge of breaking into the laptop and uncovering whatever secrets it might reveal. He was quite a nerd when it came to technology, but his skills had proven to be invaluable on several previous cases, and he was quite often consulted by other teams for his technical prowess.

"Sally, I want you to do a deep dive into Oliver Weldon and his famous pony society. There's something a bit off with him, but go carefully, he has the ear of the superintendent," Lyons said.

"I'm going to have a look at the other folks who were staying at Ocean View, and see what I can find out about the Gillespies in case there's anything there," she said.

"Right, boss" Fahy said.

When the team had dispersed to get started on their assigned tasks, Lyons withdrew to her office.

She started by calling Mrs Curley out at the guesthouse to get the Ashton's home address, and to find out how much longer they were planning to stay with her. Then she did a search on the web to find out anything she could about them.

Lyons was just getting started when Sinéad Loughran, the forensic team lead, knocked on her door.

"Got a minute, Inspector?" Sinéad said.

"Sure, come in, Sinéad, and it's Maureen by the way. Grab a seat."

When Sinéad sat down in front of Lyons' desk, she produced a plastic evidence bag with a hypodermic syringe inside.

"I did a bit of work on this," she said, holding the bag up like some kind of trophy.

"It's interesting. These things are turned out in their millions by a company in Dublin – Dun Laoghaire to be accurate. Each one has a batch number, and from that you can tell what market sector, and where, it's headed. This one went to the UK to a wholesale distributor near Manchester, and it was made about six weeks ago," Sinéad said.

"Wow. That's a lot of information, Sinéad. Well done. So, I wonder if it could have been sent back to Ireland by the distributor, or was it bought in the UK and travelled over with the killer?"

"I didn't get that far I'm afraid, but I'll see if I can get any further with it later," Sinéad said.

"Did you manage to get anything else from the syringe?"

"A bit. There are no prints on it, just smudges. I'd say whoever administered the lethal dose was wearing gloves – perhaps even surgical ones. But I can tell from the smudge pattern that the syringe was held in the right hand, a bit like a dagger," Sinéad said, holding a pencil in her right hand up over her head inside her clenched fist, "like this."

"Hmm. And we know from Dr Dodd that the needle entered Ellis's neck on the left side, so that means the killer was facing him as he delivered the deadly injection," Lyons said.

"Yes, and with Ellis unconscious, or partly at least, slumped on the ground from the whack on the head, the killer must have leaned over his prone form to deliver the poison," Sinéad surmised.

"Are you sure you didn't miss anything at the scene, Sinéad? A hair on Ellis's clothes, or a flake of skin or dandruff even – anything we could get a DNA sample from?" Lyons asked.

"I don't think so, Maureen, but I'll go over it all again just to make sure. But don't get your hopes up. My guys are pretty thorough," she said.

"I know they are, Sinéad, and I don't mean to imply otherwise, but this one's a right mystery. We're going to need some lucky breaks to crack it!"

Chapter Nine

When Lyons had the Ashtons' UK address, it made her efforts to find out about them on the web a whole lot easier. They were booked in for one more night at Ocean View, and then they were off back to England according to Mrs Curley.

Connemara ponies were not the Ashtons' main equine interest, it seemed, although they did keep one at their place in Northampton. Their main business was training and breeding thoroughbred horses, and while it appeared that their stables were a modest affair with a license for just six animals in training at any one time, they had chalked up some success about four years ago with a filly called Molly Boru, who had come first in a novice's handicap at Towcester. Molly Boru had been placed at a few more outings in the UK, but appeared to have faded into obscurity since.

Then Lyons had an idea.

She called Hays' mobile, which as expected, went through to voicemail.

"Hi Mick, it's me. Could you call me before you go off sight-seeing today? Thanks, bye."

She hated leaving messages on those things. She was never certain the person would get the message, but, she supposed, it was better than nothing.

* * *

When Hays called her back, Lyons filled him in with as much detail as she could find on the website about the Ashtons' operation. She asked him if he would be willing to drive out to their place and have a snoop around to see what he could find out.

"Sure. Give me the postcode and I'll get a car and drive out there. With them out of the way in Ireland, I'll have a chance to have a good look around," he said.

When Hays had finished talking to Lyons, he got a taxi straight into town and hired a car. The course he had been attending was taking place in a splendid old manor house hotel near Dunstable, so at least he wasn't that far from where the Ashtons had their stables and livery operation between Brixworth and Spratton. He could have used the M1 as far as Northampton and then turned off, but he was in quite a relaxed mood, so he decided to avoid the frenzy of the busy motorway, and took the A5 instead. He drove to Old Stratford, then onto the A508 through Yardley Gobion and Stoke Bruerne, skirting Northampton on the A45 and then on to the A43 past Moulton and Holcot into Brixworth.

As Hays drove along, he was impressed by the tidiness and order of the countryside. Even the smaller A roads all had kerb stones along their edges, and laybys where rural buses could pull in, unlike Ireland where the metalled surface of country roads just bled away into the grass and weeds at the verges.

In late August the countryside was a patchwork of huge brown, green and golden fields. Harvesting of wheat and barley was well underway, and he frequently saw huge machines cutting the ripened grain, throwing up clouds of dust as they filled up their trailers with tons of produce and ejected finished bales of straw at what seemed like a dizzy pace. In other fields, where the crops had already been harvested, enormous flocks of birds fed greedily on the spilled grains, gaining body weight for the winter ahead.

Hays was surprised at the dimensions of the fields he was passing. Each could easily be fifteen or twenty acres in size, unlike the fields he was used to seeing in the west of Ireland which rarely exceeded a single acre, often dotted with rocky limestone outcrops that made the use of machinery impossible. This was farming on an industrial scale, and to make the point, from time to time a large green John Deere tractor came bouncing along the road towards him towing a heavily laden trailer of ripe grain destined for the merchants where it would be weighed and dried before being ground into flour, or malted for brewing.

Soon Hays passed Pitsford Water at the edge of the country park. A cluster of small sailing boats was milling around, presumably a sailing club for children of school-going age enjoying the last of their holidays before returning to lessons in a week's time. Hays then drove on through the village of Brixworth, a pretty village with houses of bright yellow bricks and many with thatched rooves, but not much commercial activity. The village was dominated by a large church that seemed bigger than would be required by the local community, and Hays assumed it must have some historical significance.

Once he had driven through the village he found himself on the Spratton road, and after just over a mile, exactly as the sat nav had predicted, the gates to Spratton Dale Farm appeared on the left-hand side of the road. It was an impressive entrance, with tall wrought iron gates set at the back of a deep, curved stone wall leading off the road. A "Private Property" sign had been bolted onto the gates through the vertical bars, but thankfully they stood open, allowing Hays to drive in.

The driveway curved around to the left, past a paddock with stud fencing where a chestnut horse grazed lazily in the bright afternoon sunshine.

As the drive straightened out, an expansive brown brick property fronted by neatly trimmed lawns and bright pink hydrangeas revealed itself. It was clearly a barn conversion, and a very expensive one at that. All along the ground floor frontage, large windows set into broad black metal frames provided a view into the spacious lounge and well-equipped kitchen of the house. A substantial porch had been attached to the right-hand side of the property, and beyond it a good sized annex with a wooden door and three windows came back down along the side of the driveway. The upstairs portion of the house sported four of the same styled windows, although smaller than those below, again set in black metal frames. The pitched slated roof facing down the drive supported an array of solar panels.

To the left of the house the beige gravel driveway led off around the back to where the stable yard was presumably located.

Hays stopped the little rental car in front of the house and got out. He looked carefully in through the downstairs windows but could see no signs of life. He didn't bother ringing the doorbell, but instead strolled around the back of the house where, as he had anticipated, a large and pristine stable yard was found.

The yard ran parallel to the back of the house, and the stable block stood a good fifty metres back from it. The yard in between was mostly in plain concrete, punctuated here and there with squares of coloured bricks, and several drains. Six loose boxes ran along the stable block with what Hays assumed to be a tack room at the end. The rectangle was completed by a large garage with two sets of double wooden doors, closed and padlocked at the far end of the yard opposite the entrance.

Half way along the block, the door to one of the stables stood open, and scraping noises could be heard inside.

"Excuse me. Good afternoon," Hays said to the back of a young man earnestly engaged in mucking out the place.

"Oh, hello," the young man said turning to face Hays. He was a lad of between nineteen and twenty-two years of age with a mop of curly blonde hair and a ruddy face, dressed in the unofficial uniform of such folks with wellington boots, tan corduroy pants and a sleeveless green quilted jacket on top of a twill shirt.

"Sorry to disturb you. I was looking for Jack Ashton if he's about," Hays said.

"I'm sorry, sir, I'm afraid he's away in Ireland at the Connemara Pony Show. He should be back the day after tomorrow," the lad said, resting on the fork he had been using.

"Oh, I see. What's your name?" Hays said.

"Malcolm. Malcolm Fulton. And you are?"

"Oh, yes, sorry. Michael Hays. I met Mr Ashton at the horse show in Dublin at the start of August, and he said if I was ever in the area to be sure to call in, so here I am," Hays said, smiling broadly to re-assure the stable boy that he was not a threat.

"I'm sorry, but it looks like you've had a wasted journey I'm afraid. Look, I'm just about to take a break, would you like a cup of tea or something?" the boy asked.

"Thanks, that would be great, I've been driving for quite a while."

The two men headed off into the tack room where a tiny kitchenette had been set up in one corner. There was a small stainless-steel sink, a microwave oven, a very small fridge and a kettle. Half a dozen thick earthenware mugs hung from hooks over the sink. As Malcolm brewed the tea, he asked Hays, "What has you in these parts then?"

"I travel a lot with my work. I was doing some business in Dunstable and had the afternoon off, so I thought I'd pop up and see Jack and Alison," Hays said, improvising. He went on, "Have you worked here long?"

"Yeah. I started here when I were sixteen. I've been here five years now, though it doesn't seem that long. I'm not a bit academic, me. I enjoy the horses and the open air, and I get to go to lots of shows and race meetings. Suits me fine," Malcolm said, selecting two of the better mugs from the hooks above the sink and retrieving an open glass bottle of milk from the fridge.

"Do they have many horses here then?" Hays said.

"We normally have all the boxes full. But we've lost a few lately, so we only have four in training at the moment."

"Lost a few? Do you mean they went to another yard?" Hays said, pouring a measure of milk into his tea.

"Na, they died didn't they. Three of them since I've been here. Bloody weird if ye ask me, never known the like," Malcolm said.

"Right, yes, it does seem a bit odd all right. How did they die?"

"Just passed away. Found them dead in the stables in the morning. Jack, Mr Ashton, had post mortems done and all. Vet said they died of a heart attack. Happens sometimes with thoroughbreds it seems, but three in a row is right bad luck," he said.

"Who's the vet then?" Hays said.

"That's Mr Carlyle over beyond Spratton on the way to Teeton. He specializes in horses he does. Nice fella. He looks after them proper," Malcolm said.

"And has Mr Carlyle always looked after the horses here?" Hays asked.

"Oh yeah, ever since I can remember anyways."

Hays finished his tea, thanked the lad for his hospitality and made to leave.

"I'll be sure to tell Mr Ashton you called. What was your name again?"

"Ah, don't worry about it. I'll catch up with him at the next show." Hays beat a hasty retreat before the lad could enquire further.

Chapter Ten

By mid-afternoon Lyons was getting impatient to move things along. She called the team together to see what progress had been made.

"You first, John. What did you get from Ellis's PC and the cards in his wallet?" she said.

"Very little, Inspector. There are a few fairly bland emails, and some document files, again quite inconsequential. So, I've started digging a bit deeper. I popped open the cache on the laptop and found references to Word documents that aren't on the hard drive. It looks as if he had some other storage device that he plugged in and then removed for security. I have the banks digging around for information from the various credit cards, but you know what they're like, it will be a day or two before we get anything. And that membership card we found – there's no such association, it was pure fake," the young Garda said.

"Terrific. So basically, you've got nothing at all useful then," Lyons said, letting her frustration show more than was usual for her.

"Sorry, Inspector. I'll keep at it. Maybe something else will show up," O'Connor said, unhappy that Lyons appeared to be displeased with his work.

"Eamon, are you sure you didn't miss anything in his room out at Ocean View? If there's another storage device he might have hidden in the room," Lyons said.

"I'm pretty sure the room was clean, Inspector. Of course, I didn't pull up any floorboards or anything, but anyway, if I was him I wouldn't have hidden it in the room in case the nosey Mrs Curley came across it," Flynn said.

"So where would you have hidden it then, Eamon?"

"Probably in my car. That way it wouldn't be too far away from me at any time, and there would be less chance of it being discovered," Flynn said.

The others nodded encouragingly at what their colleague had proposed.

"Right, well then get onto Sinéad Loughran and get her to pull that car apart. Tell her what we're looking for and for God's sake get her to get a move on. The trail is going stone cold while we're all sitting around doing bugger all!"

"Sally. What's the news on Weldon?"

"Turns out he's quite an important player in the whole Connemara pony scene. He breeds them, and he shows up at any sort of gathering involved with the animals, and it's not just Connemaras he's into, he does thoroughbreds as well. And he's well connected too. There are lots of photos of him with the Mayor of Galway, the head of the Lyons Club, various local politicians, and even one of him at a dinner with our very own Superintendent Plunkett," Fahy said.

"All well and good, but we need to get behind all that flim-flam. Try to see if you can get any financials on him — you know, grant applications, property deals, that sort of thing. He was decidedly uncomfortable in our presence out in Clifden, and I'd like to know why!" Lyons said.

* * *

Hays left the Ashton's and headed on towards Spratton. It was a glorious day in rural England, and he was enjoying the trip a lot. He had checked the web on his mobile phone to locate Carlyle's veterinary practice, which was, as the stable lad had told him, on the far side of the village.

As he drove through the chocolate box village of Spratton, he noticed the King's Head pub on the corner with a sign hanging out announcing "Food served all day", and he decided that he would call in on the way back from the vets to sample the fare.

The veterinary practice was easy to find. A large sign-written wooden board giving details of surgery hours and proudly boasting "Vet on call 24/7/365" was fixed to the gate, and up along quite a short drive Hays could see a number of buildings. He drove in and parked in front of a long low "L" shaped building that looked as if it was the business end of the operation. Several other vehicles were parked there too. Off to the right, standing behind a beautifully manicured lawn, was a large bungalow that Hays calculated must run to well over 3000 square feet, with an expensive navy-blue Jaguar parked in front.

Hays got out and entered the low building via a door marked "Reception". Inside, an atrium with a tiled floor, brightly lit by a large overhead skylight, accommodated two reception desks behind each of which sat a dark-haired girl. The girls were both in their twenties.

"Good afternoon, sir," the nearest one said in a cheery voice, "how can I help you?"

"I was hoping for a brief word with Mr Carlyle, if that's possible?" Hays said.

"I'm sorry, sir, he's out on call just now. Can one of the other vets help?" she said.

"No, it's OK thanks. Will Mr Carlyle be back in this evening?"

"Yes, he'll be here in about half an hour for evening surgery. Would you like me to make an appointment for you?" the girl said, apparently not at all fazed by the fact that Hays didn't appear to have an animal with him.

"No thanks, it's fine. It's just a small personal matter. I'll catch him again, don't worry," Hays said.

The girl started to ask who she could say had called, but Hays made swiftly for the door and let himself out before having to identify himself. The two receptionists looked at each other and shrugged their shoulders.

Outside, Hays got back into his car and drove out of the premises. He turned right at the exit, and parked up about fifty yards from the gate in a small layby where he had a good view of any traffic entering or leaving the vet's place. Fifteen minutes later he was rewarded when a shiny, newish Range Rover came towards him going a bit faster than was sensible for the narrow B road, and turned into the gateway. The single occupant was a man in his fifties with a good crop of greying hair and dark rimmed glasses. He appeared, from what Hays could see, to be dressed in a dark green boiler suit.

Hays followed the Range Rover up the drive and intercepted the man as he was getting out of the car.

"Mr Carlyle? Sorry to pounce on you like this, my name is Michael Hays. I'm with the Irish police. I wonder if I could have a quick word with you – unofficially, of course?"

Carlyle looked at his watch and said, "Well if you can be quick, Mr Hays, I have surgery in a few minutes and I need to clean up first."

"I won't keep you long, I promise," Hays said, smiling as broadly as he could without making himself look like a total idiot.

"I understand you look after the animals over at Jack Ashton's yard," Hays went on.

"Yes. That's right. I've known the Ashtons for years. Nice people," the vet said.

"Indeed, if a tad unfortunate. I believe they have lost at least three horses in almost as many years," Hays said.

"Yes, yes they have. But there's nothing untoward going on, I can assure you. I did the post mortems on those animals myself. It sometimes happens like that. These animals are very highly bred, and that quite often throws up congenital defects which are a bugger to spot before it's too late. But it looks as if their run of bad luck is over for now anyway. Why the interest?" Carlyle said.

"Oh, you know, just pursuing enquiries. A case I'm working on back at home, a few threads pointing in this direction. But thank you for your help, and I'd appreciate it if you didn't mention my call to Jack or Mrs Ashton, it's all very much off the record you see," Hays said.

"No worries. Mum's the word. Now I really must get on," Carlyle said.

"By the way, I understand that Ashton's dead horses were all cremated. Is that normal in these instances?" Hays asked.

"Oh yes, perfectly. A horse is a very big animal to bury, so they either go for dog food, or are cremated. Mrs Ashton didn't like the thought of them ending up in tins of Lassie!"

Hays had years of experience interviewing suspects from all walks of life. He had developed a keen sense of when a person was lying to him, or at least being economical with the truth, and he could see in Carlyle's eyes that he was not being forthright.

Chapter Eleven

Maureen Lyons was still at her desk when her mobile phone sprang to life.

"Hiya Mick. How's things?" she said.

"Great. I've just had a delicious meal at the King's Head in Spratton. Roast duck with all the trimmings – mmmm."

"You bastard! I had a stale cheese sandwich at lunch and now I'm bloody starving. I'm still at work you know," she said.

Hays went on to describe the events of the afternoon and what he had discovered about the very high mortality rate among the horses at Ashton's yard.

"Do you think there's something in it?" Lyons asked.

"Well, it's a coincidence, isn't it, and you know me. I don't like coincidences. Anyway, what are you up to?"

"Trying to find out something – anything at all would be good – about the deceased. So far, apart from his name and address – nada. And I'm getting rightly pissed off with it," she grumbled. She went on to tell him about the delay in getting the banks to respond, and the presence of the fake membership card for the Association of Photographic Journalists that they had found in his wallet.

"Easy tiger. Why don't you go home and open a bottle of wine and chill for a bit? It will all be still there tomorrow, you know."

"Ah, I dunno. Home isn't the same without you, Mick. I'm as well off here causing trouble for a while longer. Can't wait to get you back to Galway though, show you what you've been missing!"

"How do you know I've been missing out on anything?" he said, teasing her.

"Just get back here tomorrow, Inspector, and don't be late!"

"Before you go, there is one angle you could try. I know one of the sub-editors on The Journal – Tom Scanlon, or "Scally" as we used to call him. He's sound, and he'll deal with you off the record if you ask him. Give him a call and see if he's ever encountered your mystery man, or heard of that photographic crowd. And tell him from me if he breathes a word, he'll have fifty speeding tickets before the month is out!" Hays said.

"Nice one, Mick. That's breakfast in bed for you on Sunday if that pans out," Lyons said.

"What? Just breakfast?"

"Well, maybe an extra grilled tomato, or a rasher then, we'll see. Go on, will ya? Text me this Scally's number. Goodnight."

Lyons' phone pinged a few seconds later and Tom Scanlon's number was inserted automatically into her contacts.

Lyons was just about to call him when Sinéad Loughran knocked on her door.

"Come in Sinéad. You look happy. What have you there?" Lyons said.

"Found it in Ellis's car. Hidden in a matchbox on the parcel shelf. Hiding in plain sight, as it were," she said beaming.

"Great. But what is it?"

"It's a thumb drive for a PC. Tiny, but believe it or not it holds 128 gigabytes of stuff. That's almost a whole PC's worth," Sinéad said.

"Cool. That's terrific. Well done you. But I think it's best to wait till John comes in tomorrow before we connect it up, unless you want to have a go? Knowing my luck with technology, I'd probably wipe the whole thing clean," Lyons said.

"Probably best to leave it till tomorrow. I'll put it in the evidence room for the night for safe keeping," Sinéad said. "Fancy a drink?" she added.

"Sinéad, there's no longer any doubt – you're officially a genius. But give me a minute, I have one phone call to make first," Lyons said.

"Oh, OK. I'll wait outside."

"No, stay where you are, it's grand," Lyons said, indicating with her hand for Sinéad to stay put, "I won't be a minute."

Lyons dialled the number Hays had sent her by text.

"Tom Scanlon," said the voice that answered after two rings.

"Good evening, Mr Scanlon. My name is Detective Inspector Maureen Lyons from Galway. I'm a colleague of

Senior Detective Mick Hays. He gave me your name," she said.

"Ah, yes, Mick, the rascal. What's he up to these days?" Scanlon asked.

"We're investigating a sudden death out here in the west, and Mick was wondering if you might have heard of our victim, David Ellis? He may be somehow connected to the bloodstock industry," Lyons said.

"Ellis, Ellis, let me see. The name seems vaguely familiar, but I can't place him. Give me an hour or two and I'll have a root around, see what I can find. Is it OK to call you later?" Scanlon said.

"Sure, thanks, Mr Scanlon, that would be great. But of course, this is completely off the record, is that all right?"

"OK, understood, and call me Tom by the way, Inspector. Any friend of Mick's, well, you know. Chat later." With that he was gone.

Lyons held the phone away from her face and scowled at it.

"Hmph. Funny bloke. But he could be helpful," she said out loud.

"OK. Let's go. I have a thirst I wouldn't sell for a tenner!" Lyons said, picking up her handbag, slipping on her navy-blue suit jacket and flicking her hair out from under the collar.

"Doherty's?" she said to Sinéad as they made their way out of the by now largely deserted building.

"Do you mind if we don't? Liam 'the groper' Dempsey from the drugs unit will be in there with his cronies, and you know what he's like. After a few pints he thinks he's God's gift. I've had to fend him off a few times," Sinéad said.

"Jesus, Sinéad. I thought he had a partner, and didn't they have a baby recently?"

"Yes, but that's all the more reason to stay in the pub surrounded by fawning young constables keen to curry favour with the more senior ranks. Beats dirty nappies and yarking babies any day," Sinéad said.

"For fuck sake, Sinéad!" Their laughter could be heard echoing through the empty corridors of Mill Street Garda station as they headed for the door.

The two women made their way across the river at Bridge Street, turned right into Cross Street and then left into Middle Street. At the corner of Middle Street and Buttermilk Walk stood an old stone-built pub called "An Béal Bocht", which is Irish for "The Poor Mouth". The ground floor of the pub was jammed with a mixture of tourists and late-night shoppers, but the upstairs lounge was still more or less empty at this hour, so they made their way upstairs.

"So, is Mick still away in the UK?" Sinéad asked when they were settled in front of their drinks in a quiet corner of the lounge.

"Yeah. He's back tomorrow, thank heavens."

"Do you miss him a lot?"

"Yes, I do to be honest. It's not just the company either. I feel safe when he's around, and I do my job better too with him there backing me up. He's got so much experience, and I have so much to learn," Lyons said.

"Seems to me you're doing pretty well, Maureen. Look at that thing last year. Not many female officers would have taken out that McWhatsit character like you did. I'm surprised they didn't give you a medal," Sinéad said.

"Ah, away with ye. That was more good luck than anything else, and McFadden wasn't exactly a master criminal."

"But I don't know about Mick and me," she went on, unprompted, "you know I've kept my flat down by the river just in case he throws me out. I have it rented to a fresh-faced young Garda just out of Templemore on a six-month lease."

"God, Maureen. I thought you and Mick were a permanent fixture," Sinéad said.

"We are, I think. But there's just something niggling me about it. Some detective I am. You'd think I could get to the bottom of whatever it is, wouldn't you?"

"I think that's cool. You don't take him for granted. There's that hint of unpredictability about it. That's good," Sinéad said.

"Anyway, enough about me. How are you getting on with James?" Lyons said.

"God, I don't know, Maureen. He has, shall we say, certain skills that are very pleasing for a girl, but he's boring. Give him a pipe, a pair of slippers and a copy of The Irish Independent and he'd never move away from the fireplace again. I'm not ready for that!"

"You'll never be ready for that girl, but it's good that you're getting something out of it," Lyons said.

"Maybe we should swap!"

"Feck off, Loughran. Anyway, Mick prefers brunettes."

"Yeah right. That's what he tells you." They both laughed out loud.

Lyons was just starting into her second glass of Cabernet Sauvignon when her phone stared chirping in her handbag. She rooted around in the bag, retrieving the phone on the fifth ring, just in time to stop it going to voice-mail.

"Lyons," she said.

"Hi, Inspector. It's Tom Scanlon. I managed to dig up a bit on your mystery man, David Ellis. I knew the name rang a bell. He used to work for the Irish Press newspaper here in Dublin, but when that folded he went freelance. Lately, he's been doing a bit of investigative stuff into crimes of one kind or another. He writes under the name Dionysus and we quite often carry some of his seedier stuff. Is that any help?" Scanlon said.

"Yes, indeed it is, Tom, that's terrific. Thank you. You don't happen to know what he was working on recently do you?"

"No, sorry, haven't a clue."

"Oh well, listen, that's very helpful, thanks a lot," she said.

"No bother, and give my best to Mick, the rascal. Bye."

Sinéad Loughran had heard both sides of the conversation with Tom Scanlon.

"He's a useful contact," Sinéad said.

"Isn't he just. One of Mick's of course — see what I mean? Anyway, your mission, Ms Loughran, should you choose to accept it, is to explore that little memory thingy you got from the car first thing tomorrow, and find out just what our Mr Ellis was up to," Lyons said.

"Oh, no pressure then."

When they had finished their second drink, the two women left the pub. Lyons wanted to get home to do a job on the house before Mick returned the following day. She had done a lot of work on the place even before she moved in, and she wanted it to be a real home for them both to act as a catalyst cementing their relationship.

On the way home, an idea came to her. Based on the information Mick Hays had shared with her about the Ashton's, she decided it would be a good idea to have them interviewed before they left the country. She didn't want to do it herself, so she called Eamon Flynn on her hands-free phone as she was driving home.

"Hi Eamon. Look I'd like you to do something for me. Could you go out early tomorrow morning to the Ocean View Guesthouse near Clifden and interview Mr and Mrs Ashton. Give them a good grilling about where they were the night Ellis was killed, and see what you can shake loose. Bring Pascal Brosnan along too if you like, to lend a bit of weight to the process," Lyons said.

"Sure, boss, that's no problem. What time do I need to be out there?"

"I'd get there around eight if you can. We don't want them doing an early one and getting away before you have a chance to speak to them. And when you've finished the interview, give me a call and let me know how it went. Is all that OK?"

"Yes, fine. I'll call you after. Bye," Flynn said, and was gone.

Chapter Twelve

Flynn left the city early to get out to Clifden by 8:00 a.m. as instructed. There was virtually no traffic at all on the road, and he ignored the speed limit, so he made good progress. He had called Pascal Brosnan the previous night and arranged to meet him at Ocean View at eight o'clock.

Although the two men were of different ranks, they tended to greet each other by their first names if no one was about.

"Hi Pascal. Thanks for coming out," Flynn said, getting out of his car on the neat tarmac driveway of the guesthouse.

"Ah, no bother Eamon. What's the drill here?"

"We just have to interview the Ashtons. Inspector Hays has been doing some investigations in the UK, and he reckons they are worth a shake," Flynn said.

"How do you want to play it?" Brosnan asked as they walked towards the door.

"Just as it comes. Feel free to join in if you think I'm missing anything."

Mrs Curley answered the door and was clearly surprised to see two policemen calling at such an early hour.

"Good morning, Mrs Curley. Garda Brosnan and myself just wanted a word with the Ashtons before they leave. Are they up yet?" Flynn asked.

"Well, you'd better come in," she said, indicating that they should go into the lounge on the right side of the hall. The lounge was very clean and tidy, and provided a large comfortable sofa and several well upholstered easy chairs, as well as a modern television and a sideboard covered in current magazines and brochures for the various attractions in the area. Flynn noticed that the embers of turf in the fire were still giving out a modicum of heat, which was why, he surmised, the grate had not been cleaned out as yet.

"If you'll just wait here, I'll tell them you're wanting to speak to them. They're just having their breakfast. Oh, and would you gentlemen like a cup of tea or coffee?" Mrs Curley asked, unable to prevent her natural hospitality coming to the fore.

"That would be very nice, Mrs Curley. Tea would be fine," Pascal Brosnan said.

Mrs Curley left them to it, hurrying away to tell the Ashtons about their visitors and prepare the unexpected additional refreshments for the two men.

After a few minutes, Jack and Alison Ashton came into the lounge and the two Gardaí introduced themselves. When all were seated, Flynn opened the conversation.

"As you know, folks, there was an unpleasant incident out at the pony show the other day in which a man lost his life. We believe he was murdered. We're talking to anyone who was there on that day, or has any connection to the deceased. It's purely routine in these circumstances."

Alison Ashton was clearly uneasy with the situation. She was seated at the very edge of her chair, and was wringing her hands together uncomfortably as the detective spoke.

"So, may I ask you about your movements on the day in question? I assume you were together for much of the day," Flynn went on.

"Yes, yes of course," Jack Ashton said. "We breakfasted here as usual. Then we went out to the show and spent the morning watching the jumping and talking to some of the competitors, and people we know from the pony club. We left at about one o'clock, and drove on out towards Westport, stopping at the viewing area in Louisburg to enjoy Mrs Curley's marvellous packed lunch," Ashton said, looking at his wife for confirmation. Alison nodded and smiled briefly.

"Then we drove on into Westport and visited Westport House. That would have been mid-afternoon or thereabouts. After that, we drove back into Clifden where we had dinner in Foyle's Hotel at around seven o'clock. Then we came back here, watched the BBC News on TV and went to bed," Ashton said.

"Did you have a reservation for Foyle's Hotel?" Brosnan asked.

"Oh, yes we did. It was very full, so we booked it the previous day, and they said as long as we would be gone by eight thirty when they needed the table, that would be fine."

"Tell me, Mr Ashton, did you know the deceased at all? David Ellis was his name," Flynn said.

"No, no, I don't believe so. Was he a breeder?"

"No. He was an investigative journalist. We think he may have been working on a case related to the ponies, or at least horses in general. Are you sure you never came across him?" Flynn asked.

"Quite sure, Sergeant. Now, if there's nothing else, we need to get packed up and be gone. We have a ferry to catch," Ashton said.

* * *

Mrs Curley brought in a tray with a large pot of tea, four cups and saucers, and the inevitable plate of home baked scones just as the Ashtons stood up. Flynn was sure she had been listening at the door and timed her entrance to disguise the fact.

When the Ashtons had gone upstairs, Brosnan went to find the lady of the house to confirm the times that Ashton had given them for the night Ellis was killed.

"Yes, that's right, she said. They came in about nine. We watched the Irish news on RTE, and then they asked if we could change channel to the BBC so they could see the English news. After that, they went up to bed," the woman said.

"And they didn't go out again at all?" Brosnan said.

"No. I would have heard them coming and going. No, they stayed in after that. Why? Is that important?

"Just making sure we have covered everything, Mrs Curley. Thanks for the tea. We'll leave you in peace now."

Once they were outside, and out of earshot, Flynn phoned Foyle's Hotel and checked that the Ashtons had in fact eaten dinner there that night.

"Oh yes. They have been in a few times, and they were definitely here that night. We were very busy, but I remember them. They left a generous tip," the girl on the phone said.

"Well, that's that," Flynn said to Brosnan.

"Was it worth the trip, Eamon?"

"I think so. Strange that they didn't say that they knew Ellis from the guesthouse. They were staying there at the same time, and they must have breakfasted together at least. And Mrs Ashton was very nervous," Flynn said.

"God, I missed that completely, but you're right. Is it significant?" Brosnan said.

"Could be, Pascal, could be."

Flynn caught Lyons just before she left the house for work and relayed the details of the interview with the Ashtons.

"That's all very well, Eamon, but what feeling did you get when they were talking to you? Did you get a sense that they were hiding something?"

"Well they denied knowing Ellis, despite the fact that he had been at the guesthouse with them, and it's not exactly palatial, so they must have met at some stage."

"Interesting. Well thanks anyway. See you later."

* * *

Lyons sat at her desk nursing a mug of milky coffee. After she had given the house a thorough clean the previous night, she had finished off an open bottle of red wine, watching some daft mind-numbing game show on TV. There must have been more in the bottle than she thought, for her stomach felt acidy, and she had the start of a thumping headache. She swallowed two paracetamols in the hope of seeing it off before it really took hold.

By nine o'clock the open plan office had filled up, so she made an effort and called the team together.

"Right, folks, we have lots to do today. I want to see some real progress before Inspector Hays gets back, or he'll think we've been on holiday too!" A murmur of subdued mirth went around the room.

"John, can you talk to Sinéad, and between you get busy with that memory stick. Get as much as you can off it, and arrange it in reverse date order – latest first. Get Sally involved if you need her, and while you're at it, get onto his bank and get them to expedite his bank statements – and I don't want to hear any of that data protection bullshit – got it?" Lyons said.

"Yes, boss," O'Connor said.

"Sally, I want you on Weldon. Again, bank statements, travel records, even bloody parking tickets. There's something not right with him. You'll need a warrant, so get the form done up, I'll sign it and then you can take it upstairs," she said. "Oh, and Sally, can you go along to the PM? I'm not feeling up to looking at dead bodies being slit open this morning."

"Sure. But about Weldon's bank accounts, wouldn't it just be easier to ask him for them, boss?" Fahy said.

"Probably. But I don't want to alert him yet, so just do it the way I asked, will you?" She realised that she was being a grumpy cow, but the tablets hadn't eased the pain in her head and she was determined to make progress before Mick returned.

"I'm going to dig around on Ellis now that we know what he did for a living. I'll get the lads in Dublin to go around to his place too and see what they can find. Let's chat again at one o'clock," she said.

Lyons retreated to her office and started trawling the net for any articles she could find concerning, or written by, Ellis. It didn't take long for her to get lucky. There were a number of pieces featuring Dionysus. The stories featured a lot of fairly low-level crime where Ellis had brought wrong-doers to book when the Gardaí had been unable to do so due to the constraints under which they were operating. Ellis was able to use entrapment and infiltration, and he was able to do some other illegal stuff too that led to the exposure of criminals involved in fencing stolen property or car theft. Once the criminals were caught, Ellis would sell the story to the papers or TV stations who love this kind of stuff. It seemed he was careful to avoid anything involving organized crime though, probably in case they decided to take revenge on him.

"Well that didn't work out too well, David, did it?" Lyons said to no one at all.

She was just starting down another rabbit hole on her PC when the phone on her desk jangled.

"God, that bloody thing is loud today," she thought, reaching for the instrument.

"Lyons," she said.

"Maureen, good morning, it's Superintendent Plunkett. I wonder if you could spare me a few minutes in my office?"

"Yes, of course, sir. Now?"

"Thanks, yes, now would be fine," he said and hung up.

Lyons had a good idea what this was about, so she rehearsed a few lines as she climbed the stairs to the third floor where Plunkett had his relatively plush office. Before Lyons had properly sat down in front of his very spacious and clutter free mahogany desk, Plunkett began to speak.

"Look, Maureen, I'll get straight to the point. I see you've requested a warrant to see Oliver Weldon's bank accounts. Is that really necessary? I know Oliver, quite well as it happens, and I very much doubt that he's involved in anything shady, let alone murder," Plunkett said.

"Yes, sir, I understand. But we need to cover all the bases on this one. I'm sure you're right, but I need to be thorough."

Even as she said it, she knew it sounded weak.

"This isn't the first time you've gone after an acquaintance of mine who turned out to be totally innocent, is it, Inspector?"

Lyons knew that he was referring to James McMahon, and architect from Galway who had been investigated in connection with the Lisa Palowski murder out on the old bog road, near Ballyconneely a few years back.

"Well, yes, sir. But it did look as if he could have been involved, and he was visiting an escort regularly if memory serves."

Lyons was determined not to roll over for the superintendent too easily.

"Hmph. Well anyway, what's your interest in Mr Weldon?"

Lyons went on to explain that she was fairly certain that Ellis was investigating something that was going on to do with the bloodstock business, and as Weldon was top and tail of the event where the man met his death, she felt the need to investigate. He wasn't the only person of interest that they were looking at.

"Oh, very well then, I'll sign it off, but I'm not happy. Not a bit happy. This better lead to something, or there will be consequences. Dismissed!"

"Jesus," thought Lyons as she made her way back to her office, "I wonder how much raw meat he had for breakfast. Her headache was back – well, in truth, it had never really gone away. She felt like shit.

Back in her office she started looking through her PC again to see what else she could find out about Ellis. She had only just got started when a dark shape filled her doorway. It was Superintendent Plunkett.

"Maureen, I need you with me now. Get your jacket, and hurry up," he barked.

By the time she had locked the screen on her computer and picked up her jacket from the back of the chair, Plunkett was already disappearing down the corridor.

* * *

Lyons sat back in the plush beige leather of Plunkett's Audi A6. She had never been in the Super's car before and she loved it. The dashboard was walnut and there seemed to be all sorts of gadgets at the disposal of the driver and passenger, as well, of course, as fully automatic climate control. The big engine purred sweetly, even though he was pushing it along fairly hard.

"Where are we going, sir?"

"Out to Bearna. Oliver Weldon's disappeared, and poor Laura is beside herself with worry," he said.

Lyons knew she had to tread carefully here after their earlier exchange. On the one hand she felt somewhat vindicated by the situation, but she also felt that Plunkett could easily blame her for Weldon's disappearance. It was completely ridiculous, but you didn't get to be Superintendent in the Gardaí without learning how to pass the blame for the things that went wrong onto the lower ranks.

Before she had time to frame a tactful question, the superintendent went on.

"He got a phone call about five o'clock yesterday and said he had to meet someone out west. Laura was out at Bridge last night and when she came home she went straight to bed and didn't notice he wasn't home until this morning," he said.

"And she doesn't know who the phone call was from I suppose?"

"You suppose correctly, Inspector," he replied, and pushed the sleek black car on a pace towards Bearna.

Bearna is a thriving village community that lies to the west of Galway city, out past Salthill on the Galway Bay coast. It used to be a small, sleepy place – just a few houses and shops – on the way to Spiddle, but in recent times it had grown substantially. The village is officially designated as part of the Gaeltacht, or Gaelic speaking region. As a result, to encourage population growth, or rather to stem de-population, Galway County Council allowed much more lenient planning consent in the area, and soon after they had relaxed the rules, very large houses began to spring up between the narrow coastal road and the shoreline. The wealthy tradespeople of Galway had taken full advantage of the position, and several properties with indoor swimming pools, gymnasia, and other unlikely features, all running to over 5000 square feet, had appeared in the area. Weldon's was one of these. It stood on the rocky, boggy ground to the left of the R336, and enjoyed spectacular views of the Atlantic Ocean from the back of the property. A low, flat-roofed building, so designed to minimize the impact of the prevailing westerly wind during the stormy winters, the house was ultra-modern in style and maintained in immaculate order.

As Lyons got out of the Audi she noticed a slight autumnal coolness on the breeze, and she could see that the heather was now in full bloom – a sure sign that winter wasn't far away.

Chapter Thirteen

Laura Weldon was in a bad way. She had obviously been crying, and couldn't stand still, prancing up and down wringing her hands.

"It's all right Laura," Plunkett said, "we'll find him. It's probably just something perfectly simple. Don't fret." Then, as an aside to Lyons, he went on, "Could you rustle up some tea, Maureen, and while you're out in the kitchen, call the station and get another female officer out here pronto. Get her to bring a telephone recording device in case there's a ransom demand," he said.

"It's not like Oliver at all. He always keeps in touch," the woman said, near to tears again.

"What happens when you call his mobile?" Plunkett asked her.

"It just goes straight to voice-mail. It must be turned off," Laura said.

"Have you tried texting Oliver?"

"Yes, of course, Finbarr, but there's been no response," she said.

"Have you any idea exactly where he was going, Laura, and who he was meeting?"

"No, he didn't say. But I'm sure it was something to do with the horses. It always is with Oliver. God, I hope he's OK."

Lyons came back into the lounge carrying a tray with a large teapot, three mugs, a jug of milk, a sugar bowl, and a plate of biscuits.

"Here, Laura, have a cup of tea. Have you eaten anything yet this morning?" Plunkett asked.

"No. No, I couldn't eat a thing, but thanks for the tea, Inspector," she said, managing a half-smile.

"It's Maureen, call me Maureen, Mrs Weldon," Lyons said.

As Laura Weldon poured out tea for the three of them, Finbarr Plunkett caught Lyons' eye and indicated that they needed to go into the kitchen to talk.

"We just have a few things to arrange, Laura, we'll be back in a minute," Plunkett said, but Laura Weldon hardly noticed. She was in a little private world of her own, and on this particular day, it wasn't a very nice place to be.

In the kitchen, out of earshot of Laura Weldon, Lyons was first to speak.

"Mary Costello is on her way out, sir. She's in my car, so as not to alert anyone. She has the recorder with her. We've put out an alert on Weldon's car. We got the details from the motor tax office. What else do you need?" Lyons said.

"I need you to get out to Clifden as soon as you can. Take my car, it's quicker. It has a siren, but don't use it unless you have to. I'll use yours when Mary gets here. On the way out get Mulholland lined up to have a good look around the town discreetly. When you get there, co-ordinate it, and see if there's any sign of life at the show grounds. Report back to me when you have things moving. Oh, and Maureen, if you know any good prayers, start saying them now!" he said.

* * *

Lyons decided that the quickest way to get to Clifden was to turn off at The Twelve Hotel, drive up past the Father Griffin Monument, out past Bearna Golf Club and pick up the N59 half way between the city and Moycullen. The road was narrow and boggy, but the big Audi soaked it up, and she managed a good pace with no other traffic of any kind to get in the way. She did have to use the car's siren in Moycullen where both sets of traffic lights always seemed to be set at red, but after she had cleared the village she gunned the car, and was soon hitting 130kph, though the speed limit was only 80.

"I could get used to this," she said to herself, taking the time to explore some of the toys the luxury car provided. Before Oughterard she called Sergeant Séan Mulholland in Clifden on the Audi's hands-free phone.

"Séan, it's Maureen. Have you heard about Oliver Weldon?"

Although superior in rank to Mulholland, Lyons found it better to continue to call him by his first name, as she had done while they were both sergeants. Mulholland seemed to enjoy the lack of formality, and responded well to it.

"Yes, Maureen. It came in about twenty minutes ago, and before you ask, I have Jim Dolan and several uniformed men out scouring the town for any sighting of him or his car. He's well known around here, so if he's in the area, someone will have seen him," the sergeant said.

"Great, Séan. I'll be there in twenty minutes or so, then I want to go to the show ground. Can you get someone to meet me outside?"

"Yes, of course. I'll get Peadar Tobin to wait outside for you, unless you want us to go in ahead of you?" Mulholland said.

Lyons remembered Tobin from the day Jennifer Gillespie went missing. He was a uniformed Garda in his mid-thirties, around six feet two inches tall, and well built. He was quite attractive too, in a rugged, country sort of way.

"Thanks, Séan, he'll do nicely, but get him to wait outside for me. Talk later," she said, finishing the call.

Once Lyons got through Oughterard, the scenery and the road quality changed dramatically. The weather had become overcast, suppressing the glorious blues of the distant Twelve Pins that the sunshine brings out, but the wildness of the terrain still stirred something in Maureen as she sped along towards Clifden.

"Here we bloody go again," she said to herself, "I should move out here permanently I spend so much time on this road. I must get a better car though, this is fantastic," she thought, patting the car's dashboard affectionately. In what seemed like no time at all, she was barrelling down past the new holiday cottages at Clifden Glen on the outskirts of the town.

* * *

When Lyons pulled up outside the show ground in Clifden, Peadar Tobin was standing at the gate with his hands behind his back looking like a sentry on guard duty.

"Good morning, Inspector," he said tipping the peak of his Garda cap, "nice car you've got there. Is it new?"

"Morning, Peadar. No, it's Superintendent Plunkett's. He lends it to me for long journeys so that I don't get too tired," Lyons said. The uniformed Garda didn't quite know what to make of that, so he said nothing.

"Can we get inside here, Peadar?" Lyons said.

"Well, I don't have a key, and it's padlocked. But if you turn away for a minute or two, we may find that it's actually been left open," the young garda said.

"Jesus!" Lyons said, shaking her head, and looking down the street away from Tobin.

A moment later Tobin said, "Here we go," pushing the gates open sufficiently to admit them both.

The show ground was completely deserted, with the Classic Car Show being over and nothing else planned for a week or two. They made their way quickly to the buildings, and while the door at the bottom of the stairs leading to the office was locked, there was no sign of anyone, or any evidence that there had been anyone there recently.

"Do you want me to open it?" Tobin said, "it's no bother."

"No, leave it for now, Peadar. There's no sign that anyone has been here, and if they broke in, they'd hardly go to the trouble of locking it again anyway. Let's have a look in the outbuildings," Lyons said as they made their way in that direction. Tobin walked behind her, not through any sense of chivalry, but in that way, if someone sprang out to attack her, he wouldn't have to turn around to go to her defence. Lyons recognised and appreciated his thoughtfulness.

The outbuildings were not secured – there was nothing in them worth stealing – but it would be an ideal place to hold someone secretly, so the pair were thorough in their search. They looked in all of the stables, in the tack room, now bare of any equipment, and the sluice room which had been cleaned down and now smelled of Jeyes Fluid, with a few small pools of the murky liquid still drying out on the concrete floor. The two officers then walked around the paddock, but found nothing other than a few discarded drinks cans and some empty potato crisp wrappers.

Just as they were leaving the show grounds, Lyons' phone rang.

"Maureen, it's Séan here. I've just had a call from Pascal Brosnan out in Roundstone. They've found Weldon's Mercedes on the little road leading down to Gurteen. It's parked in the entrance to a site, and the builder can't get his JCB in, so he reported it," Mulholland said.

Pascal Brosnan was the single Garda who ran the police station in Roundstone. Miraculously, the village had been spared the devastating cuts following the financial crisis in 2011 when hundreds of rural Garda stations had been closed in an effort to save money. Brosnan was a bachelor who lived in a modern bungalow not far from the Garda station, and he had proven to be most useful the previous year when a young visitor to the area had been kidnapped.

"OK. Thanks, Séan, I'm on my way," Lyons said.

Lyons left Peadar Tobin to walk back to the station and set out along the old bog road towards Roundstone in Plunkett's car. By this time, she knew the road well and was able to cover the distance to Gurteen in fifteen minutes. When she drove down the little lane that led to the caravan site and the beautiful white sandy horse-shoe shaped beach of Gurteen Bay, Pascal Brosnan was lounging against Weldon's apparently abandoned car.

"Hi Pascal," she said getting out of the Audi, "Is it locked?"

"Yes, Inspector, and the engine is cold. Looks like it's been here for a while," Brosnan said.

"Have you had a look around? Any sign of the driver?"

"No, not yet. I was waiting for some backup," the young Garda said.

"Right. Well I'm here now, so let's see what we can find."

Unlike Tobin had in Clifden, Brosnan went ahead of Lyons, and pushed open the flimsy makeshift wire gate that was guarding access to the site where yet another bungalow was being constructed. After a few minutes searching fruitlessly, Lyons decided on some more positive action.

"Pascal, can you get on to Séan and get him to send as many people as he can spare out to us as soon as possible. We're going to have to comb out the whole area till we find Oliver Weldon, assuming he's here somewhere. I'll get onto Superintendent Plunkett and get him to mobilize a crew from Galway," Lyons said.

She called Plunkett's phone, but got no reply, so then she phoned the Weldon's house and asked to speak to Mary Costello.

"Hi, Mary. Anything there?"

"No, Inspector. All quiet here. What about out where you are?" Costello said.

"Well, we've found Weldon's car, but don't say anything to Mrs Weldon just yet. Is the superintendent there?"

"No. He left in your car about half an hour ago. He has a lunch engagement with a visiting delegation of French police. It seems they are here to find out how we handle rural policing."

"Shit. So, can you get onto Mill Street and get them to mobilize a team of five or six and get them out here pronto on my instruction. We'll have to start a search for Oliver Weldon, if he hasn't been spirited away somewhere else altogether," Lyons said.

"Do you think he's still alive, Inspector?" Costello said.

"I bloody hope so, Mary, I really do."

Chapter Fourteen

By mid-afternoon a team of uniformed Gardaí were swarming all over Gurteen Bay. They looked at every bungalow, and searched the caravan site, looking in, and even under, each of the static mobile homes, in the toilet block and washrooms, and even in the vehicles used by the park's owners, but there was no sign of Oliver Weldon anywhere.

At almost four thirty an odd thing happened. A shiny black Ford Granada hearse came slowly down the track leading to Gurteen with a small group of elderly mourners walking sombrely behind it. The men were dressed in old, well-worn two-piece suits, and each of them had a cap perched on his head. The only two women in the cortege wore heavy tweed coats and had head scarves. Lyons saw the hearse approaching and called Pascal Brosnan aside.

"What's this Pascal?" she said.

"That's old Festus O'Rourke. He died in the nursing home at the weekend. His family are all buried here in the graveyard up on the hill that separates Gurteen from Dog's Bay."

"Well, ask the men to keep well out of their way, will you?"

"Sure. They won't be long putting him in the ground anyway. They've already said Mass up at the church."

The small, sad procession continued along past the car park at the beach, and stopped at the gates leading into the graveyard. The undertakers manoeuvred the pale oak coffin out of the back of the hearse, and led by the priest – dressed in black and white robes with a black biretta and a silk stole embroidered in gold and purple – the little group made their way awkwardly into the cemetery where a fresh grave had been dug out of the rocky ground. The grave was covered by a light wooden frame with an artificial grass mat over it, to conceal the black hole beneath. Two gravediggers appeared from nowhere, and as the undertakers put the coffin down, they threaded strong canvas straps through the handles in preparation for the burial. They then removed the wooden frame from over the grave and stopped in their tracks.

Staring up at them from six feet below the surface of the ground was none other than Oliver Weldon. He had silver duct tape across his mouth, and his hands and feet were bound tightly with more of the same. As soon as the daylight reached him, he stared blinking rapidly and moving his arms, wriggling about as much as the confined space would allow, and grunting, fearful that he might be taken for dead and be buried alive.

As soon as the shout went up, several uniformed Gardaí ran to the graveside expecting the worst. Lyons' radio crackled into life with an excited voice shouting, "We've found him. He's in the grave, but he's alive!"

"Christ Almighty, what next!" Lyons said as she ran off towards the graveyard with Pascal Brosnan at her side.

* * *

It took the combined skills of the two gravediggers, two strong Gardaí and the priest to extricate Oliver Weldon from his tomb. After all, graves normally only experience one-way traffic, and the damned thing was almost six feet deep. Eventually Weldon was brought to the surface, feeling very weak and very cold. So much so that he couldn't speak coherently, even after the tape around his mouth had been rather painfully removed. He was shaking uncontrollably. They sat him on the coping stone of another nearby grave, and one of the Gardaí gave him his jacket while another was despatched to the caravan site to procure a mug of warm sugary tea. Tea, it seems, in the west of Ireland can even bring people back from the grave!

Lyons called Mulholland and asked him to get an ambulance there as quickly as he could, explaining where and in what condition they had found Mr Weldon. Then she tried Superintendent Plunkett again, and this time got through.

"Jesus Christ, Maureen. What the hell is going on?" Plunkett said on hearing where and how his friend had been found.

"Look, sir, he'll be OK. He's had a truly horrific ordeal, and he's cold, weak and very hungry, but he's alive. The ambulance is on its way. I thought you might like to tell Mrs Weldon yourself, sir," Lyons said.

"Yes, thanks Maureen, I'll call her now. And when you've tidied up out there I want you to come back in and see me. I'll wait in my office till you arrive, and besides, I need my car back," Plunkett said.

"Yes, sir, of course, sir, and I'll be needing mine back as well," she said, not wanting to let him get the upper hand completely.

"What? Oh yes, of course. I had to put fuel in it you know, it was right out."

"Excellent," she thought to herself smiling, "and I won't be putting any diesel in yours, mate!"

Lyons felt that there was little point in trying to turn the grave into a crime scene. There had been too many people hoofing around, and there was no material that could hold a decent fingerprint anywhere about, although she did bag up the duct tape just in case. She told the priest he could proceed with the burial. The small group that had come to see Festus O'Rourke to his final resting place all appeared to be totally numbed by the whole episode, but Lyons had no doubt that the story would be told, and probably enhanced, in the pubs in Roundstone that evening, and eventually make it into the local folklore.

Lyons imagined what they would say: "And when they went to put poor old Festy in the ground, wasn't there some other fella already in there. And I wouldn't mind, but wasn't he only alive!"

"If this is going to be my last trip in Superintendent Plunkett's car, I'm damn well going to enjoy it!" she said to herself as she approached Roundstone village. She flicked on the switch for the siren and went screaming through the village as fast as she dared, much to the amazement of the locals. And then on to Recess, and Maam Cross pushing the Audi all the way. In the late afternoon, the clouds had given way to bright sunshine, and the long shadows from the mountains along with the purple of the heather all over the boggy land made a genuinely beautiful panorama as she drove along. She made good time until she encountered the evening traffic on the Newcastle Road, and as if to signal the end of her adventure for the day, a heavy shower descended making the road slick and her humour grey like the clouds overhead.

Just as Lyons was pulling into the car park at Mill Street, her phone rang. It was Mick Hays.

"Hi, where are you?" he said full of cheer.

"Hi, Mick. I'm just getting back to the station. I have a meeting with the Super. Where are you?"

"I'm at home. Do you think you'll be long?"

"No, I doubt it. Plunkett will be keen to get away, but I'll have to keep him here for a few minutes till his car cools down," Lyons said.

"What?"

"Never mind, I'll tell you later."

"Why don't we meet in O'Conaire's at, say, seven thirty. You can tell me all about it then. Oh, and leave the cars, I need a drink," Hays said.

"Great. See you there."

Superintendent Finbarr Plunkett was restless when Lyons arrived into his office.

"Come in, Maureen, give me an update," he said.

Lyons outlined the events of the day from the time she had left the Superintendent out at Bearna.

"Do you think he'll be OK?" he asked when she had finished.

"Well, physically, he'll be fine. He wasn't hurt. But it may take him a bit longer to get over it mentally. That was quite an ordeal."

"You're telling me. What's this all about, Maureen?" he said.

"I'm not sure yet, but we will get to the bottom of it, sir, don't worry."

"Do you think the two incidents are connected?" the Superintendent said.

"It's too early to say, but it's definitely a possibility. I'll know more tomorrow when we have more information about the dead man, sir."

"Is Mick back yet?"

"He's just arrived home."

"Good. Get him to go and see Oliver in the morning. I want Weldon to know that we're taking this very seriously," he said.

Lyons bristled with the imputation, but bit her tongue. Plunkett was in no mood to be challenged.

"May I have my car keys please, Inspector?" Plunkett said.

"Oh, yes, sorry, sir," she said, handing them over somewhat reluctantly and collecting her own car key from his desk.

"By the way, sir, how did you get on with the French contingent?" Lyons said.

"It was a bit mad, to be honest. They didn't really speak English, and I don't do French, so it was all a bit stilted. I don't think they were too interested in rural crime at all – more of a junket I'd say. But at least the brought me a nice hamper of good French wine and cheeses," the superintendent said.

"It's well for some," Lyons said to herself.

Chapter Fifteen

When Lyons got to O'Conaire's, she found Mick Hays sitting at the bar with a half-finished pint of Guinness in front of him. He got up when he saw her and the two embraced for a little longer than was appropriate given the location. When Lyons eventually withdrew, she had a tear in her eye. Hays saw it, and took her in his arms again and held her close, saying, "Hey. It's OK, love, it's OK."

She finally stood back and said, "For pity's sake Mick, will ye get me a drink?"

"That's better, tiger! What's your poison?"

Lyons spent the next half hour filling Hays in on the events of the day. He listened intently without interrupting until she had finished the story.

"And to top it all off, he wants you – Mr Senior Inspector – to go and see Weldon in the morning. Apparently, I'm not up to it!" she said.

They ordered their favourite meal as they sat in the window upstairs in the restaurant looking out over the calm water of Galway docks. A coaster, looking far too big to fit in the cramped harbour, was manoeuvring up against the quayside to collect a load of scrap metal that had been processed in one of the factories in the industrial estate adjoining the pier.

"Anyway, enough about me. How was your training course?" Lyons said.

"Better than I thought to be honest. The first day was a bit boring, but on day two they focused on the future, and the plans that they had to gear up the whole digital crime detection area. A chief superintendent gave us a talk," Hays said.

"Cool. Anything we could use?"

"Probably. But it's only at the planning stage for now. They're setting up a new unit in London. He even asked me if I'd be interested in heading it up. Apparently, they had done a good deal of investigation into my background before I arrived," Hays said.

"Jesus, Mick. Leave the Guards and transplant yourself to London? What did you say?" Lyons studied his face, and in particular his eyes, as she waited for his response.

"I thanked him for his kind offer and said I would give it some serious thought," Hays said after a moment or two.

Later, after they got home, they went to bed and made love, but it was purely perfunctory. A physical release, lacking any real passion or emotion. As Hays drifted off to sleep, Lyons turned her back to him. "Damn it, I'm losing him," she said to herself, and quietly cried herself to sleep.

* * *

The following morning Hays phoned the hospital from his office and was told that Oliver Weldon was to be discharged as soon as a doctor had seen him at about eleven o'clock. His wife was coming in to collect him, so they should be back home in Bearna by noon.

Lyons called John O'Connor into her office and was being updated on what had been discovered about David Ellis, the dead man, the previous day while Lyons was busy dealing with the Weldon incident.

"As we know, Ellis was an investigative journalist. In the last few years he had worked on a number of crime stories, employing techniques denied to the police, and had been instrumental in the arrest of some pretty big names, leading to successful prosecutions. Most of these were white collar crimes – fraud, tax evasion, money laundering and so on," O'Connor said.

"I see. Any idea what he was working on just now?"

"Well the Dublin lads found a notebook in his apartment that may give us a clue, but it doesn't mean much to me," he said.

"What about the memory stick?" she said.

"Not much there. Bank statements. A few fairly bland letters. Some budgeting spreadsheets, and a few drafts of old articles that he must have had published, but nothing current," O'Connor said.

"What do the bank statements tell us?"

"All the usual stuff. Rent payments, utility bills, that sort of thing. Cash withdrawals mostly from ATMs, and sporadic in-payments by bank transfer of quite decent sums, presumably when he got paid for his work. Oh, and there's a monthly payment of €1000 going to another bank as well."

"Could be a loan for a car or something," Lyons said.

"That's a bit rich for a car loan, boss, and anyway wasn't he driving an eight-year-old jalopy that we found out in Clifden?"

"Yes, I see what you mean. Follow that up. See who's at the receiving end, and then collate everything relevant into a folder. Include the notes from the notebook and leave it to me, John, thanks," Lyons said.

"Already done," O'Connor said producing a red plastic document folder and handing it to the inspector. Lyons studied it. Her instincts took her to the jottings that had been found in Ellis's Dublin flat. On one page, there were a series of what could be disconnected jottings, but Lyons was nevertheless intrigued.

"TGNS 6393", "Ashtons", "3 deaths", "Carlyle".

Before she could process the information, O'Connor was back at her door.

"Sorry, Inspector, you asked me to do a bit of a background check on Oliver Weldon, so I did."

"And?"

"Well, it's all much as you would expect – pillar of the community, well connected, lots of charity stuff – but there is one odd thing. He appears to have at least eight bank accounts, two in England," O'Connor said.

"That's a bit odd all right. What age is he? He looked about a hundred and fifty when we got him out of the grave."

"He's fifty-two, and no children."

"Is Laura the original wife?" Lyons said.

"Yes. They married when he was twenty-eight. She was a successful show jumper – she still does a bit, but it's mostly dressage these days."

"And how does Weldon make his money? Let me guess – horses."

"Exactly. He breeds them and trades extensively in thoroughbreds, and the Connemaras too. But the real money is in the thoroughbreds. He's been quite successful," O'Connor said.

Before Lyons had a chance to look any further into the notes on Ellis, Hays appeared in her doorway.

"I'd like you to come out with me to see the Weldons in Bearna," he said.

"But Plunkett said you were to do it."

"He didn't specify I was to be on my own, and anyway, I'm not having you cut out like that – it's your case, you should be in on it," Hays said.

"OK, cool. Let's go," she said, taking her jacket from the back of her chair and grabbing her handbag off the desk.

On the way out to Bearna, Lyons asked Hays if he had thought anymore about the job offer from the UK.

"Haven't had a chance to be honest. And I'd have to make sure they could find a good spot for you too," he said.

"Don't worry about me. I could probably get a job at the checkouts in Asda or something," she said in a rather caustic tone. But they didn't have time to pursue the conversation as they had just arrived at Weldon's palatial spread.

When Laura Weldon answered the door, Lyons introduced Hays giving him his full title, and they went inside. Oliver Weldon, looking better than he had the last time Lyons had seen him, but still tired and drawn, was sitting in a large comfortable armchair positioned so that he could look across the bog to the sea through the large picture window.

Hays shook hands with the man and told him not to get up. Laura Weldon offered the two detectives tea, which they willingly accepted. They were happy to have her out of earshot for the questions they were about to ask her husband in any case. Hays got straight to the point.

"Mr Weldon, Superintendent Plunkett has asked me to take personal charge of this very serious incident. He sends his best wishes to you by the way. We need to ask you some questions about the incident itself, and what you believe may have been behind it."

"Well I can tell you what happened, certainly, but I have no idea whatever was behind it, no idea at all," Weldon replied.

Lyons felt he was a little too certain, and she noted that he looked down at the floor as he delivered the last part of the sentence.

"I received a phone call at about five o'clock the day before yesterday. The caller was well spoken with a British accent, and called himself Roger Williams. He said he was in the market for a young thoroughbred filly and had heard that I might be able to help him. He asked me to meet him at the caravan site at Gurteen, saying that his wife had taken the car into Galway," Weldon said.

"Do you often get that type of unsolicited enquiry, Mr Weldon?" Lyons asked.

"Not often, but it does happen sometimes. That's the business I'm in, and I'm quite well known. Most of my transactions are concluded at organised sales at Goff's or somewhere, but it's not unusual to get such an approach," the man said.

"Very good. Go on, sir. What happened when you got to Gurteen?" Hays said.

"Well I was driving down the narrow road to the car park at the beach. About two thirds of the way down, the lane was closed off with three traffic cones, and two men were standing there indicating that I pull over to the side. I thought it was something to do with the building going on there, so I pulled the car across the site entrance. As soon as I'd stopped the car, the door was wrenched open, and I was dragged out and one of them put tape across my mouth and bound my wrists. It all happened so quickly," Weldon said, clearly not enjoying having to recall his treatment.

"Did either of the men speak?" Lyons asked.

"No. Not at that time, Inspector, but later on just before they, well you know." His voice was breaking up and he was visibly shaking as he recalled what had been done to him.

"Go on," urged Hays, "what happened next?"

"Then they bundled me off across the fields and up into the graveyard, and we stopped beside an open grave. I was terrified. I thought they were going to bury me alive!" Weldon half sobbed.

"Did you struggle with them, Mr Weldon?" Lyons said.

"Yes, of course, at first at least. But they were very strong, and there were two of them after all, and they had bound my wrists with that dreadful tape. Anyway, I was frightened for my life!"

"Did you get a good look at them?" Lyons said.

"Not really. They both had black woolly hats on pulled well down, and jackets with high collars. One was taller than the other though, and they were both wearing builder's boots. I think maybe one of them might have had some sort of tattoo on the side of his neck though, but I couldn't make out the shape."

"So, what happened at the grave?" Hays said.

"The taller one said 'This is just a warning for you. Don't say nothing to nobody, or next time we'll fill the bleeding grave in on top of you. Got it?' And then they bound my ankles with that tape and pushed me in. I landed on my front, and had to wriggle around to get on my back, just in time to see them putting the cover over, and then they were gone."

"Very nasty. Very nasty indeed," Hays said.

Mrs Weldon came in carrying a tray with four bone china tea cups and saucers and what looked like a solid silver teapot. There was an Irish linen tray cloth, a silver milk jug, a matching silver sugar bowl with cubed sugar and a little silver tongs, and, inevitably, a plate of homemade buns.

Lyons took the interruption as an opportunity to go outside. Her first call was to Sinéad Loughran. She asked Sinéad to go out to Gurteen and do a forensic search of the area between where Weldon's car had been found and the graveyard.

"Anything at all, Sinéad. They may have dropped cigarette ends while they were waiting for Weldon to arrive. And look for boot prints going away across the fields up behind the site. Weldon says they went up that way to get into the graveyard," Lyons said.

Next, she called detective Eamon Flynn in Mill Street.

"Eamon, I want you to organise two or three uniformed Gardaí to go out to Gurteen and question the locals about the incident there involving Oliver Weldon. Someone must have seen something. Get Séan Mulholland to volunteer Jim Dolan as well. I want every house and caravan knocked up. Oh, and just on the off chance, see if anyone bought a roll of strong duct tape in Roundstone earlier in the week. There were two blokes, possibly British. Rough looking men by all accounts," she said.

"What about the Ellis case, boss? John has dug up some more information," Flynn said.

"OK, good. I'll be back in before long and we can pick it up then. Let's have a briefing at, say, three o'clock."

Hays decided not to persist with any more questioning of Oliver Weldon. Of course, there was more to be told, but instead of pushing it with Laura present, he asked Weldon to come into the station the following day to make a statement. "While it's still all fresh in your mind," Hays said.

On the way back to town Lyons decided not to raise the sensitive topic of Hays' recent career opportunity. She would save that for later when they were alone, and had time for a proper row.

Chapter Sixteen

When Lyons got back to the station she called Sally Fahy and John O'Connor into her office.

"Right, John, what have you found out about our victim?"

"Quite a bit. From the notebook the Dublin lads got from his flat, I may have been able to make a link to the pony show," O'Connor said.

"Go on."

"Well that reference TGNS 6393. It's a Lloyds Insurance Syndicate in London. Treadwell, Galbraith, Newton and Smythe, and they specialize in insurance for all kinds of horsey stuff. You can even insure against your stallion firing blanks," he said.

"Thanks, John, a little too much information if you don't mind," Lyons said, "is that it?"

"No. He had the name Jack Ashton in the notebook too, and an odd entry, 'Molly Boru'. I looked up Molly Boru. She was a horse that won a few races in England as a two-year-old. Jack Ashton trained her," O'Connor said.

"Hmm. Interesting, and then our Mr Ellis ended up in the same guesthouse as Jack Ashton during the week of the show. More than a coincidence?" Lyons said.

"I'd say so," Sally Fahy said, "why don't I give that Lloyds crowd a call and see what I can find out?"

"Good idea, Sally. Anything more from Ellis's bank records?"

"Yes. That €1000 a month payment goes to a Nicola Byrne. I'm getting an address for her now," O'Connor said.

"OK, good work. Sally, let me know when you've spoken to the Lloyds crowd – what was it again, TGNS?"

"Yes, that's it," Sally said.

* * *

The girl that answered the phone when Fahy called the number in London, which she had found on the web, spoke in a very posh, home counties English accent.

"Treadwell, Galbraith, Newton and Smythe, good morning, how may I help you?"

"Hello. I am Detective Fahy from the Irish police. I wonder if I could speak to one of the partners please?"

"Well, Gregg Newman is our managing agent. May I ask what it's in connection with and I'll see if he's available?" the posh girl said.

"It's a confidential police matter, so if you could just put me through please," Fahy said in the most assertive tone she could muster. The line went dead, and for a moment she thought that she had been cut off, but a few seconds later a man answered.

"Newman," he said in an equally up-market accent.

Fahy explained who she was.

"I wonder if you could tell me, Mr Newman, if your syndicate has any connection to a horse called Molly Boru?"

"My dear detective, we deal with over two thousand horses here. I can't possibly remember them individually by name," he said with more than a hint of petulance.

"Oh, sorry, yes of course. Well does the name Jack Ashton ring any bells?" Fahy asked, determined not to be put off.

"Ashton. Oh, yes, I remember him all right. His yard is insured with us. He's up Northampton way if I remember correctly," Newman said.

"Yes. Brixworth or Spratton I think," Fahy said.

"Look, detective, do you mind if I call you back in a few minutes? I'd just like my secretary to get out the file so that I know what I'm talking about."

"That's fine, thank you, Mr Newman, that would be very helpful," Fahy said and gave the man her number.

It was twenty minutes later when Gregg Newman called her back.

"Thanks for calling back, Mr Newman. Did you get the Ashton's file?" Fahy asked.

"Yes. I wanted to be sure we were talking about the right stable. Now, what is it that you'd like to know?"

"I was just wondering if there was anything unusual in your dealings with the Ashton's yard, sir?"

"Well, I'm not sure if I should be telling you this, but yes there is. Ashton has put in large claims for three dead animals over the past four years. Of course, his insurance premiums have gone up, but he's definitely on the right side of it for now. To be honest we are quite concerned, and we have employed our own firm of investigators to look into it. But all the deaths were properly certified by a qualified vet, so we had to pay out. May I ask what your interest is?" Newman said.

"We're investigating a suspicious death over here and the Ashton's name just came up during our enquiries, but there may be no connection. We're just following up leads," Fahy said.

"I'm sorry to hear that, but I'm not sure how we can help."

"Well what you have told me so far is very useful. Do you mind if I ask who your investigator is?"

"They're a firm we use from time to time. They have good connections in racing and breeding. You can call Peter Hackett." Newman went on to read out a very long UK mobile number that Sally Fahy took down carefully.

"Just before I go, may I ask how much you have paid out to the Ashtons?" Fahy said.

"I'm sorry, detective, that's strictly confidential, but I can say it has been well into six figures – so far," Newman said.

When the call was finished, Fahy tried the UK number for Peter Hackett, but there was no answer, and it went through to voice-mail. She didn't leave a message.

* * *

Hays had a message on his desk to call Superintendent Plunkett as soon as he got in. Plunkett's secretary answered the phone and demanded Hays' presence in the superintendent's office.

"Come in, Mick, take the weight off. Did you see Oliver?"

"Yes. He's a bit shook up, but there's nothing broken other than his pride," Hays said.

"Look, Mick, this is very awkward for me. I don't want your people going around digging up all sorts on Weldon. He's very well connected, and not without influence further up the food chain. Just see if you can catch the buggers that assaulted him and leave it at that, will ye?"

"Well, OK, sir, but I think you should know that there are a few aspects of his background that warrant looking into," Hays said.

"Such as?"

"Such as he appears to have at least eight bank accounts, and there may be a connection to a UK breeder that we're also looking at in connection with the Ellis murder," Hays said.

Plunkett stirred his substantial frame restlessly in his seat.

"For fuck sake, Mick, eight bank accounts is hardly a crime, now is it? And of course he has connections to UK breeders. He's doing business in the Middle East too, but that doesn't mean he's a card-carrying member of ISIS!"

The superintendent had gone even redder in the face than usual and was clearly very agitated.

"OK, sir, we'll go easy, but if he's mixed up in anything crooked, it will come out. These things have a habit of coming to the surface, you know," Hays said.

"Ah sure, don't you know the whole horse thing is just one big cess-pit – it's as crooked as a ginnet's prick! Just don't embarrass me. I hear there's a vacancy for a sergeant coming up on the Aran Islands and I wouldn't like you to have to apply for it!" Plunkett said.

"You needn't worry about my future," Hays muttered under his breath.

"What's that?"

"Nothing, sir. Is that all?"

"Yes, away with ye, and tell that girly of yours to keep her nose out as well now, do you hear?"

Back in the open plan, Hays signalled to Lyons that he wanted to see her in his office.

"Jesus, Plunkett's going mad!" he said.

"What's wrong with him? Did he find out that I'd been speeding in his car?"

"Worse than that. It's Weldon – he's a friend of his of course, wouldn't you know."

"Well, unhappily for the superintendent, it may not be that easy to leave his friend out of things," Lyons said.

"How do you mean?"

"While he was in hospital, I got the Garda that was watching him to go through his stuff," Lyons said.

"Jesus, Maureen. You do like living dangerously, don't you!"

"Yeah, well, upstanding pillars of the community don't usually end up in the bottom of a freshly dug grave, do they?"

"Fair point. What did you find out?" Hays asked.

"Well a second mobile phone for starters. I got the cop to note down the number, and I've pulled the phone records. Mr Goody-two-shoes Weldon has been calling Ashton's yard regularly over the past year," Lyons said.

"But that could be perfectly innocent, surely," Hays said.

"It could. But Sally has found out that Ashton's insurers have been investigating him in connection with the horse deaths you found out about. C'mon Mick – if it quacks like a duck…"

"Damn it, Maureen, if this goes pear shaped Plunkett will tear the arse out of both of us," Hays said.

"Sure, what do you care? You'll be away to your fancy new job in England, won't ya?" she said and turned away, walking out and leaving Hays slightly dumbfounded.

"Maureen, Maureen, wait," he called after her, but she kept going.

Chapter Seventeen

Out at Gurteen Bay, fluffy cotton wool clouds scampered across the sun leaving light and dark patches on the calm blue water. Sinéad Loughran had arrived with two more white-suited members of her team, and they were carefully inspecting the area where Oliver Weldon's Mercedes had been found for clues to the identity of his abductors.

Jim Dolan had arrived in from Clifden too, and along with Flynn and two other uniformed Gardaí, they were searching among the long stringy grass in the field leading up to the graveyard.

They had been searching for an hour or more when an old man in a greasy grey suit buttoned in the middle of the jacket, wearing a cap over his tanned and weather-beaten head, came down the lane. His progress was aided by a long stick he had in his left hand, and he was accompanied by an unkempt black and white collie dog who held its head low, with a wild look in its eyes.

The man stopped alongside Loughran's white 4x4, but said nothing. Sinéad wandered over casually.

"Hello there. We're out looking for evidence of an assault that took place here a few days ago," she said.

"Ye mean the fella in the big car?" the old man said.

"A Mercedes, yes. I don't suppose you saw anything out of the ordinary that day, did you?" Loughran said.

"Ah, no, sure I don't come around here much. Unless of course you mean the van," he said.

"Van. You saw a van?"

"Aye. A big silvery grey thing with a yellow number plate at the back. It was here for about an hour," he said.

"What time was this when you saw the van?" Loughran asked.

"I don't bother too much about time, Mrs. My watch broke a few years back. But it was quite well on in the day," he said.

"Could it have been the builder's van?"

"Not at all. Sure isn't their van white, or it would be if they ever washed it?" the man said, breaking into a smile revealing that he only had about four crooked yellow teeth in his mouth.

"Did you get a look at the occupants at all?" Loughran said.

"Aye, I did. Two fellas they were with woolly hats. A bit rough looking, so I stayed well clear."

"I don't suppose you remember the number of the van?" she said.

"Not a bit of it! Sure, why would I be bothered with that sort of thing?" he said.

"Oh well, thanks for your help in any case. I must get on," she said.

And with that, the old timer continued on past them down to the beach, the dog trotting ahead of him to chase away a few seagulls from the water's edge.

* * *

It was late afternoon when the team got together again for an update on the murder, and the assault on Oliver Weldon. Hays left it to Lyons to run the meeting, so she stood at the front of the room alongside the whiteboard adorned with photos of both of the victims and other miscellaneous information.

"Right, everyone. Let's see what we've got then," Lyons said, calling the meeting to order. "John, you first."

"Thanks, Inspector. Well I'm afraid the USB key yielded very little, but I did get some more information from the bank. The monthly payment made by Ellis goes to a Nicola Byrne. I managed to find some records for a person of that name, and it looks as if she and David Ellis were married at some stage. There's no record of a divorce, but Ms Byrne, her maiden name incidentally, has been living at her current address for a good few years now," O'Connor said.

"I see," said Lyons, "so the monthly payment is possibly alimony then."

"Yes, in all probability," O'Connor confirmed.

"Does Byrne live alone?" Fahy said.

"I haven't got that far yet, Sally, but I have an address, so it should be easy enough to find out," O'Connor said.

"Well stay on it, John. Let's see if there's anything there, although I doubt it to be honest," Lyons said.

"And you asked me to look at Weldon's travel movements. I contacted both ferry companies operating between here and the UK. Weldon uses Stena Line, and they were able to give me details of several round trips over and back to Wales," O'Connor said.

"And there's more. They told me that if you're crossing with a live horse in a horsebox, you have to book it as freight. They load those into a different area of the boat, where there's a tap so you can give the horse a drink of water, and not much fumes. If the horsebox is empty, you just book it as a passenger car and trailer, and it goes in with all the others. Weldon went over several times with a horse in the trailer and came back a few days later with an empty horsebox," O'Connor said.

"Well that's hardly surprising, that's the business he's in after all," Hays said.

"You're right of course, but there's something niggling me about it all the same. Don't you have to register a change of ownership every time you buy or sell a thoroughbred?" Lyons said.

"Yes, you do. The authorities are very strict about it," Hays said.

"John, tomorrow I'd like you to check out two things. Firstly, see if there is a change of ownership registration that coincides with each of those trips. And then get back onto the Lloyds syndicate, TGNS I think they're called, and get the exact dates for the deaths of Ashton's horses. See if there's any correlation. Our man Ellis may have been trying to join the dots," Lyons said.

"Eamon, have you anything from Gurteen?" she asked.

"Very little, boss. Sinéad found a few boot prints down at the building site, and the same ones up at the grave side in the freshly dug out soil, but they're as common as muck," Flynn said. A collective groan went around the team.

"There was a sighting of a van with a yellow rear number plate seen around at the time of the assault though," Flynn went on, trying to redeem himself. "No index mark noted, and no other sightings in the area. The two occupants match Weldon's description, such as it was, so it looks as if they were the assailants. I've put out a 'stop and arrest' bulletin for the van."

"Is that it?" Lyons asked.

Then Hays spoke up, "Oliver Weldon is coming in tomorrow morning to make an official statement about what happened to him. I think we should use the opportunity wisely, don't you, Maureen?"

"Definitely. Eamon will you and Sally take his statement, but make it more of an interview without looking obvious. He'll probably be happy enough to talk about his achievements, so let him ramble on – see what you can pick up," Lyons said.

Before they broke up, Lyons reminded them that the primary focus should be on whoever it was that killed David Ellis. Everything else was secondary, though it did look as if there could be some connection between the murder, the Weldons and the Ashtons.

When the meeting ended, Hays and Lyons headed off to Hays' office.

"Hang on a minute, there's something I forgot to do," Lyons said, and went back to catch Sally Fahy before she left the office.

"Sally, did you get in touch with that investigator the Lloyds syndicate used – Hackett I think his name is?" Lyons said.

"I called the number, but there was no reply. I'll try again now," Fahy said.

Hays looked up as Lyons came back into his office.

"Home?" he said.

"No. Tonight, DCI Hays, I am going to treat you to a posh dinner in the Great Southern Hotel. We need to talk!"

Chapter Eighteen

The penthouse restaurant in the Galway Great Southern Hotel was well known for its *haute cuisine* and very impressive wine collection. It was expensive, and often not completely booked out, and Hays knew the head waiter well, so the pair were shown to a quiet table for two with panoramic views out across the city, looking tranquil in the fading autumn twilight.

They studied the extensive menu in silence, and in the end, let the head waiter order for them. It was simpler, and they both knew that they would not be disappointed by his choices. When they had settled into a fine 2015 Saint-Émilion, Hays asked, "Well then, what's this in aid of, Maureen?"

"Guess?"

"OK. You're pregnant."

"Get lost, Hays. You know very well what this is about," Lyons responded.

"Oh, you mean my UK job offer? Well to be honest I haven't given it much thought."

"Liar," she said, but not aggressively.

"Well what do you think about it then?" Hays said.

"Oh no you don't. This is your gig. You tell me."

"Fair enough. Cards on the table. It's a terrific offer. Look at things here, Maureen. Plunkett isn't going anywhere anytime soon, and by the time he does I'll be too old for the Super's job. They may expand our team a bit, but that's about as far as it goes. The UK job is new and exciting. God knows where it could lead. The money's great, and it's something I'd like doing as well," Hays said.

"So that's it then. Game over for Galway," she said.

"No, of course not, but the way I'm feeling just now, I'd need a pretty compelling reason to turn it down."

"What about your partner?"

"Partner, what partner? Oh, you, you mean?"

"Yes, Mick. You know, the woman who shares your bed and whom you occasionally confide in," Lyons said.

"Well, I'm assuming you'd come too. I'm sure I could get you a posting in the UK as at least a DI or maybe even DCI."

"And how well do you really think that would go for me? An Irish woman parachuted into a senior position over the heads of blokes who had been thinking of little else other than promotion for God knows how many years? And another thing. Please don't make assumptions about what I'm thinking. Talk to me – I don't bite. Well, only occasionally," she said.

"Would you not want to come with me?" Hays said.

"Mick, be in no mistake, I always want to be with you. Why, even over the last few days with you away on your course I've been like a lovesick schoolgirl. So, I'll probably go with you if that's what it takes, but I'm not sure if I could hack it. I'm a Galway girl, born and bred, and if I have a choice, I kinda want to stay that way."

Just then the starter arrived, and the meal proceeded largely in an uneasy silence. They tried some meaningless small talk, but it didn't really work. When they had finished their food, Maureen paid the bill and they drove home to Salthill.

Once indoors Maureen announced, "I'm going to sleep in the spare room tonight. I have some thinking to do." Hays knew better than to argue.

Lying in the freshly made up bed in the smaller bedroom at the back of the house, Maureen Lyons lay awake pondering her fate. Her head wouldn't settle. It was a maelstrom of conflicting thoughts and feelings. When at last the dawn started to push the darkness of the night away, for the second night in a row, she silently cried herself to sleep.

Chapter Nineteen

The two thugs that had thrown Oliver Weldon into the open grave believed that they had got clean away with it. They had stopped on a quiet stretch of road between Roundstone and Recess and removed the UK number plates from the Transit van, and put back the Donegal plates. They took their time driving back, stopping over on the outskirts of Sligo, lying low for a couple of days to let things settle before going home.

They were heading up the N15 between Sligo and Donegal making sure to keep within the 100kph speed limit when they rounded a bend and saw a police checkpoint straddling the road. They had no time to turn the van around, or take any other evasive action, so they pulled up at the blue and white "STOP. Garda Checkpoint" sign propped up at the side of the road. A young Garda approached and signalled the driver to open the window.

"Good morning, men. Where are you headed this morning?" the young Garda said.

"We're on our way back to Donegal, Garda, we've been down in Sligo doing a bit of work," the driver said.

"Oh, right so. Do you know that your insurance is out of date?"

"What? Oh no, Garda, it's been renewed, I just haven't got round to putting the disc in the window yet. I have it at home."

"Just pull the vehicle over to the side please, and we'll sort it out," the Garda said. They driver complied, and pulled the van onto the hard shoulder.

The Garda opened the door of the van to speak to the driver about the insurance, and noticed two yellow number plates sitting on the floor of the van between the two occupants. He said nothing about that, but asked them if the insurance had been renewed with the same company.

The driver assured him that it had. At this stage the young officer asked them to wait in the van while he checked something out. He took possession of the van's keys as he walked away out of earshot.

He used his radio to contact his Garda station.

"This is Clancy here, sarge, I have a couple of lads stopped out here on the Donegal Road. They're in a silver Transit reg number one zero Delta Lima three six nine four zero two. But there's a set of UK plates on the floor of the van too. They are Golf November Zulu five two nine eight seven. And I don't think they have insurance either. Can you look it up on the system for me?"

"Sure, Darragh, stand by," the sergeant said.

A few minutes later Darragh Clancy's radio crackled to like.

"Darragh, are you receiving?"

"Yes, go ahead, sarge."

"You were right, the boys have no insurance, and those UK plates belong to a stolen Ford Mondeo lifted in Strabane a month ago. And Galway has a bulletin out looking for a couple of lads that sound like these two. I think you'd better bring them in for a chat."

"Right, sarge. We'll wrap up the checkpoint and bring them on in."

Garda Darragh Clancy broke the news to the two thugs in the van who were not happy, but decided not to try and make a run for it. Clancy had two other Gardaí with him and it would have been a senseless gesture in any case, and only have made their situation worse.

"What happens to our van?" the driver said when he realised that he wouldn't be driving it away.

"It will be driven into the station by one of us here, and it stays there until you can produce an insurance certificate and proof of ownership for it," Clancy said.

The two were driven away in the white Garda van that was standing by at the roadside for just such an occurrence. When they got to the Garda station, they were booked in and told they would be charged with driving without insurance and being in possession of stolen property at least, and that they would be held in a cell until further enquiries could be made.

＊ ＊ ＊

"Galway," Sergeant Flannery said, picking up the telephone. Why was it that it always rang just when he was about to enjoy a cup of tea and a few chocolate biscuits in the middle of his shift?

"Sergeant Flannery. This is Sergeant Paul McQuaid from Sligo. You have a bulletin out for two lads driving a silver van, is that right?"

"Hold on a second now, Paul, I'll have a look for you. There's so many of these blessed things these days, it's hard to keep track. Do you have names?"

"No, not yet, we've only just brought them in and they're saying nothing. Got them at a roadside checkpoint for no insurance, but there seems to be a bit more to it," Paul McQuaid said.

"There usually is! Yes. Here we are, wanted in connection with an assault on a man out at Gurteen three days ago. Ye did well to collar them, Paul. Hold on I'll put you through to the detectives and they'll know what to do," Flannery said.

Eamon Flynn took the call from the front desk and wasted no time in bringing the news to Lyons who was seated at her desk bringing the paperwork on the case up to date.

"That's great news, Eamon. Will you take Sally and get on up to Sligo and sweat the buggers? Lay it on good and thick. Talk about attempted murder – life in prison – you know the drill, and tell them we have several witness statements that put them at the scene and hint at forensics too – see if you can frighten them into telling us what's this all about," Lyons said.

* * *

Sally Fahy enjoyed Eamon's company, although there was no physical attraction there at all. Eamon was a good cop and had taught her a good few things in her first couple of years as a detective in the unit. He was a tenacious man, who never let anything rest until he had brought it to a conclusion, a trait that had served the unit well on a number of recent cases. At thirty-three he was just the right age for a detective sergeant, but he himself harboured ambition to get an inspector's post if one ever became available. He had even contemplated a transfer to another area of the country to fulfil his ambition, though he had kept that little nugget of information to himself.

"I think there may be trouble in paradise," Fahy said out of the blue as they settled in for the two-hour journey between Galway and Sligo.

"What? You mean the Mick and Maureen happy family show?" Flynn said.

"Yes, the same. I overheard them having words yesterday when Mick got back from England, and she's been a grumpy cow ever since he left for the course – and don't you dare say anything about PMT!" Sally Fahy said.

"What? Me, never. Could be though, couldn't it?" Flynn said.

Fahy whacked him as hard as she could on the leg, and he pretended to be mortally wounded.

"The sooner women take over the entire force the better if you ask me," Fahy said.

"Are you sure? There's one recent female appointment that didn't turn out too well, did it?"

"And what about the men that 'didn't turn out too well'?"

"Strange, I never rated you as a flagrant feminist, Sally," Flynn said.

"Some detective you are, sure don't you know Maureen and I have secret bra burning ceremonies at her place every weekend?"

"Nice. Can I get a ticket – that would be worth seeing!"

"Feck off Flynn, pervert," she said, and they both laughed out loud.

* * *

When they got to Sligo, they introduced themselves to Sergeant Paul McQuaid who offered them refreshments. They had a cup of tea with him, and he explained how the sharp-eyed Garda Clancy had spotted the yellow plates on the floor of the van when he stopped it to check its insurance.

"We get a fair bit of nonsense going on with cars and other vehicles being so near the border here. Fellas don't want to pay the tax bringing Northern Ireland or UK cars into the Republic, and they're inventing ever more ingenious ways of getting around it. Maybe Brexit will put an end to it. But Clancy is a good man, and he's well up to them."

"That was handy. Be sure to thank him for us, it's quite a breakthrough," Fahy said.

They went on to explain the assault on Weldon, and told the sergeant that they would be putting the fear of God into the two men in an effort to get them to tell what lay behind their adventure in Gurteen.

"Do you need any help with that?" the sergeant asked.

"Ah, no, you're grand. We're well used to the likes of them in Galway," Flynn said.

Eamon Flynn and Sally Fahy interviewed the two suspects for nearly three hours, but got absolutely nothing at all from them. It was clear that they were from that part of Donegal that borders the North of Ireland, and after the long session, the two detectives concluded that the boys may have been put up to their attack on Weldon by someone with subversive connections, and it would be more than their lives were worth to talk. They threatened, cajoled, played good-cop/bad-cop and used every other trick in their armoury, but still couldn't get a word from either of the men.

They were both wrung out after their long interrogation session, and eventually, Fahy phoned Lyons to put her in the picture.

"OK, Sally. Don't worry, I think you may be right about their connections in the North. Just have them charged with actual bodily harm and all the stuff to do with the van and the stolen plates, and leave it at that."

Lyons relayed the events of the day to Hays who went in search of the superintendent to tell him the good news – that they had two suspects in custody for the attack on his friend Oliver Weldon.

"Excellent, Mick, well done. That's a weight off my mind, I can tell you. I'll tell Oliver the news and line him up to identify the scum-bags, so we can get a conviction. It should be good for two years or more in Mountjoy at least."

"But what about the motive for the attack, superintendent? We need to follow that up, surely."

"Ah, now listen, Mick. We have the two boys who assaulted him. Isn't that good enough for you? We can't go wasting time on stuff that might be going on in England or the North – that's someone else's problem. Let's just see if we can wrap up the Ellis killing without starting World War Three and be done with it, do you hear me?"

"Yes, sir, loud and clear. There are some ongoing threads to the investigation that I'd like to see completed, but I understand your position, sir," Hays said.

"Good man, Mick. That's the spirit."

Chapter Twenty

Oliver Weldon arrived at Mill Street Garda station bright and early the following day. At the front desk he asked for Senior Inspector Michael Hays. The desk sergeant used his desk phone for a moment, and then said to Weldon, "If you'd like to come with me, sir. Inspector Hays has been called out for something urgent, but detectives Flynn and Fahy will look after you," he said, ushering the man into a small, rather dingy interview room.

A few moments later, detectives Sally Fahy and Eamon Flynn entered the room. It took them a few minutes to put Weldon at his ease. They explained that all they needed was an account of what had happened the day he was assaulted. As he started to tell his story, with Flynn writing it all down meticulously, Fahy started to broaden out the discussion.

"It must be a fascinating business you're in, Mr Weldon. I suppose you get to travel all over?" she said.

"Well, it's mostly to the UK, though I have been further afield on occasion. We sold a couple of thoroughbreds to the Middle East last year, and I had to arrange air transport for them and fly down with them. They get treated better than first class passengers on those flights you know," Weldon said.

"I'm always seeing Aidan O'Brien and Dermot Weld on the telly," Fahy said.

Weldon laughed briefly.

"We're nothing like as big as either of those two of course, but we have had our moments."

"Didn't you breed that two-year-old filly Molly Boru?" Fahy went on. She noticed Weldon flinch slightly at the mention of the horse's name, but he recovered quickly.

"Well not really. I sold her at a young age to a stables in England. But how do you know about Molly Boru?"

"It's just such a memorable name – a combination of Molly Bloom and Brian Boru. I suppose it's difficult to think up original names for them all," Fahy said.

"Yes, it is, but we get a lot of help from Wetherby's with that. They always have some good suggestions."

"I suppose they all have to be registered. Don't they all have passports or something these days?" Fahy probed.

"Yes, it's all very sophisticated, and getting more so all the time. They're even talking about a DNA database for thoroughbreds, but it's a way off yet," Weldon said.

"Why would they need that, sir?"

"Just for positive identification, like the police use for evidence."

"Yes, but your horses aren't likely to commit any crimes, are they?"

Everyone laughed.

* * *

Oliver Weldon finished the statement, read it through and signed it. It had been easier than he thought it would be, and the two detectives seemed nice enough, and very interested in his business. Once he was outside, and well clear of the Garda station, he took out his mobile phone and dialled one of his contacts.

"It's me. I've just come from the local police station. Look, we'll have to lie low for a while. There's a lot of attention on me at the moment, and I don't like it. Let's leave things for a month or two, OK?" he said.

"Fine," the female voice at the other end said. "Call me when you want to resume."

* * *

Lyons was at her desk responding to emails when her phone rang. It was the switchboard. They had an insurance company on the line who wanted to speak to someone about the David Ellis death.

"Sure. Put them through," Lyons said.

"Inspector Lyons, how can I help you?"

"Good morning, Inspector. My name is Warner from Consolidated Life and General in Dublin. I understand that you're the officer in charge of the investigation into the sudden death of Mr David Ellis," he said.

"Yes, that's right. How can I help?"

"We've had a claim in with regard to a life insurance policy we hold on Mr Ellis. It's a bit of an odd one, so I just thought we should have a word," Warner said.

"I see. In what way is it odd, Mr Warner?"

"Well, firstly, it's paid up. That is, there are no further premiums being paid on the policy, but the cover is intact for another eight years," he said.

"I see. Is that all?" Lyons said.

"No, it's not. The claimant is a Ms Nicola Byrne. It seems she was married to Ellis at some stage, and they never actually divorced, so she says she has a legitimate right to claim."

"And how much is the policy worth, Mr Warner?"

"It's €100,000, so you can see my concern."

"Yes, but why do you think this might be a police matter?" Lyons said.

"I understand Ellis was murdered, is that correct?"

"Yes, that's a matter of public record."

"Well, as I'm sure you can guess, Inspector, my company doesn't like paying out large amounts, and if there's anything fishy about the claim we are entitled to hold off till the matter is resolved," he said.

"Surely you're not suggesting that the claimant had anything to do with the death of Mr Ellis, are you, Mr Warner?"

"I'm not suggesting anything, Inspector. It's just that this falls well outside the norms of our claims experience, that's all. Have you any likely suspects for the murder?" he said.

"I'm not in a position to discuss that, Mr Warner, it's an ongoing investigation," Lyons said.

"Mmm, well I think we have enough to decline the claim, or at least delay the pay-out. We can always make a payment later when you have apprehended the guilty party. Perhaps you'd let us know when someone has been charged," Warner said.

"Perhaps."

When the call was over, Lyons went next door to tell Hays about it.

"That's a bit odd, I suppose. Maybe we should go and have a chat with Ms Byrne. What do you think?" Hays said.

"We could always let the Dublin boys look after it," Lyons suggested.

"No. I think we should go ourselves, besides, we could both do with a night away from here – clear our heads."

* * *

The team met again at lunchtime before Hays and Lyons set off east to Dublin. Fahy and Flynn brought them up to speed on the Weldon interview. Lyons was particularly interested in the information they had gleaned about animal passports. At the briefing O'Connor said that he had checked the change of ownership records against the travel days when Weldon had taken live horses to the UK.

"He made twelve trips altogether in the past three years. There are changes of ownership showing from Weldon, mostly to Jack Ashton, but not exclusively. But for two of the trips, there's nothing. So it looks like he took two horses out of the country, and, well, they disappeared!" O'Connor said.

"What about Peter Hackett – did you contact him," Lyons asked Fahy.

"I left a message. He's going to call me back later," she said.

* * *

It was a fine autumn afternoon when Hays and Lyons set off east out of Galway on the N6 towards Dublin. Once they were well clear of the city, traffic was light enough, and they made good time. There were a number of lorries travelling back to Dublin having dropped their loads out west, and the inevitable collection of tourists driving their hired Hyundai and VW Polo cars rather precariously along at well below the speed limit. In the fine weather with just a few high, scattered clouds, and with the sun almost directly behind them, driving conditions were excellent.

On the way to Dublin the conversation between them turned once again to the issue of Hays' job offer to head up a digital crime unit in the UK.

"I'm really sorry about last night," he said.

"That's OK," she said.

"No, it isn't. I spoiled a lovely meal, and I upset you as well, and that's not OK. I'm sorry."

"So, what are your plans? When do you have to let them know?"

"Listen, Maureen. I love you – very much indeed. And I can see that you don't want to leave Galway, and I fully understand that. So, I'll just put any thoughts of moving to the UK out of my head. You're more important to me than that job," he said, reaching over to take her hand in his as they drove along. Maureen was silent for a few minutes.

"I'm not sure that will work, Mick. If you turn down this opportunity, you may regret it for a long time to come, and that regret could easily turn to resentment towards me. And it could even be justified," she said.

"That's not me, Maureen. I don't hold things up my nose, you know that. Let's just let it go and carry on. I'll tell them thanks, but no thanks. It probably wouldn't have worked out anyway."

"I'm not sure, Mick. Don't say anything to them for a few more days. Let me think the whole thing through a bit more. I'm serious now," she said.

"OK. We'll park it for now then." He squeezed her hand gently.

Chapter Twenty-one

Nicola Byrne lived in a small cottage in Ringsend. The house had once been occupied by workers from the vast Pembroke Estate. But the estate had been broken up many years ago, and now these small but substantially built properties were all privately owned. Byrne's cottage was in a long unbroken terrace of fourteen similar dwellings that had no front gardens, their entrances opening directly onto the footpath. But it was a quiet road, and when the two detectives arrived in the early evening, children were out playing football and chasing all along its length.

Nicola Byrne answered the door of number eleven herself. She was a woman in her forties with a neat figure that fitted well into her blue jeans and grey T-shirt, and her long mousy coloured hair was tied in a single plait that fell down across her left shoulder. The detectives were invited into the single reception room, and sat down on the newish-looking brown leather sofa.

"How can I help you?" Byrne asked after she had offered tea which they declined in unison.

"I understand you were once married to a Mr David Ellis, Ms Byrne," Lyons began.

"Still am, as far as I know, although obviously we're not living together any longer."

"Yes, of course. You'll be aware that Mr Ellis was unfortunately found dead out in Clifden in suspicious circumstances," Lyons went on.

"Yes, yes it was terrible. I hope he didn't suffer," the woman said.

"How long have you been apart?" Hays asked.

"Let me see, it's almost five years now, yes, that's right, it will be five years in October."

"May I ask if it was an amicable separation?" Lyons said.

"I suppose it was really, in the way these things go. But it wasn't easy for either of us," Byrne said.

"No, of course not. I don't wish to pry, but may I ask why you decided to split up?" Lyons said.

"Nothing specific. Neither of us was having an affair or anything. We just lost interest in each other and neither of us wanted to go on living a lie," Byrne said.

"I see. I understand Mr Ellis had a life insurance policy," Hays said.

"Yes. David was always good at that sort of thing. He was insured for €100,000, and was paying the mortgage on this place, bless him."

"And do you live alone now, Ms Byrne?" Lyons asked.

"No, not any more. Aidan moved in last year and we're together now. I'm not good on my own."

"Aidan? May I ask his full name?" Lyons asked.

"Doyle, Aidan Doyle."

"And what does Mr Doyle do for a living?" Hays said.

"He's a maintenance man. He does work for a number of factories and warehouses out on the industrial estates, you know, electrical work, that sort of thing."

"Sorry to have to ask you, Ms Byrne, but can you tell me where you both were the night Mr Ellis was killed?" Lyons said.

"Here, both of us. We were here in the house," she said.

"I see. Just the two of you? No neighbours in for a while or anything, and you didn't go out?" Hays said.

"No. We just stayed in and had a take-away from the Chinese on the corner," Byrne said.

"OK. Well thank you very much for your time, Ms Byrne. We'll be in touch if there's anything further." They both got up to leave.

"Just one last thing. What kind of car does Aidan drive?" Lyons asked.

"A VW Golf van. It's pretty old now. He'll probably change it when the insurance money comes through. He does very high mileage in it."

"Well, thanks again," Lyons said shaking Nicola Byrne's hand on the doorstep as they left.

"What did you make of that?" Hays asked as they drove off towards the hotel they had booked for the night out at Lucan on the Galway Road.

"I think Nicola Byrne has more to tell, Mick. And that guy Aidan seems to be punching a good bit above his weight. She's a very attractive woman," Lyons said.

"Tomorrow, when we get back, let's get Eamon to do a thorough background check on both of them," Hays said.

* * *

After they had eaten a nice meal at the Spa Hotel in Lucan, Hays and Lyons went upstairs. This time there was passion and emotion in their love making, and Lyons felt a lot happier.

Maybe things might just work out, she thought.

* * *

They left Lucan at six-thirty the following morning so that they would hit Mill Street around nine, or maybe a bit earlier if Hays pushed on a bit. He wasn't given to excessive speed, but on this occasion he could always claim to be on police business if he was pinged by a speed camera, so he let the car out on the virtually deserted road. When they got to Galway, they still had time to have a hearty breakfast and be at their desks before the rest of the team arrived.

"John, I'd like you to do a good thorough background check on one Aidan Doyle, maintenance man, or so his partner tells us, and a Nicola Byrne also known as Nicola Ellis. They live together in Pembroke Cottages in Ringsend. See what you can dig up," Hays said as the morning briefing got underway.

"Sally, did you manage to contact Peter Hackett by any chance?" Hays said.

"Yes, I did indeed. What an interesting man," she said.

"Yes, I'm sure, but can we just stick to the edited highlights for now?"

"Sure, sorry, sir. He told me that he has spent a good deal of time investigating Jack Ashton over the deaths of his horses at Spratton Dale Farm. He told me there's definitely something iffy going on there, but try as he would, he was unable to find any actual evidence. He said it would have been a lot easier if the dead horses hadn't been cremated, but he eventually had to call it quits, and the syndicate very reluctantly paid out. He has a theory about what's going on, but maybe you'd rather hear about it later, sir?" Fahy said.

"Yes, later, Sally. Thanks. Do you think he might be amenable to doing a bit of sleuthing for us if it came to it?" Lyons asked.

"I think he'd love it."

Chapter Twenty-two

"Maureen, can you talk to Sally about Hackett's theory. I have to go upstairs to update Plunkett?" Hays said when they were back in his office.

"Sure. Good luck!"

"Well, Sally, tell me all about Peter Hackett's theory on the Ashtons," Lyons said a few minutes later, having called Fahy into her own office.

"It all sounds a bit farfetched to me, boss, but he thinks there's an identity swap going on."

"How would that work?" Lyons asked.

"Ashton has a horse in his yard. It has a good pedigree, but is a bit of a donkey as far as racing is concerned. These animals aren't worth a whole lot. They usually end up as show jumpers or even just pets, and they don't fetch a lot of money. Apparently, some animals just aren't into racing while others love it. So, Weldon sources a horse in Ireland that has not much breeding, but is a keen and quick racer. He has a very good eye for a young horse with potential, and he can pick them up for relatively little money. He keeps the animal for a few months and brings it on, then he transports the animal over to Ashton and they swap the horses' identities. Now Ashton has a good race horse with a fabulous pedigree, probably worth upwards of 100k, and of course there's now a spare horse. So, he kills off the spare, and claims on insurance. Between them, they pocket a right wedge of cash. He then sells on the newly created pedigree racer for big bucks and makes more money, which again he presumably shares with Weldon," Fahy said.

"But what about DNA and all that?" Lyons said.

"Apparently it's only in its infancy here and in the UK. And besides, Ashton is clever. He sells them on to little known trainers out in the sticks that run the animals at local meets. The new owners are so delighted to have a winning horse, they don't look too closely at the background. In any case, Hackett says, quite a few mistakes get made in the breeding records. There are over two million animals in the system, and it's far from watertight. And besides, everyone loves a winner, don't they?" Fahy said.

"But what about the vet and the post mortems?"

"Well, either he's in on it, or it's being done very cleverly. Hackett reckons it could be sodium chloride poisoning," Fahy said.

"What? Salt!"

"Yes, just ordinary salt. In moderate doses, it's essential for a horse's health, but in very large doses it can kill the animal, and it's not a very nice way to go it seems. But oddly, it's very hard to detect post mortem, and even if it was found, it's easy to explain away as an accidental overdose," Fahy said.

"Does Hackett think the vet is involved?"

"He doesn't know. There doesn't appear to be any other suspicious activity associated with his practice, but who knows?" Fahy said.

"Has anyone alerted the British police?" Lyons said.

"Hackett said he tried that, but they were completely disinterested. He got nowhere with it," Fahy said.

"OK, thanks, Sally, I'll talk to Mick about it and see where we go from here," Lyons said.

* * *

"How did you get on with his Lordship?" Lyons asked Hays when he re-appeared.

"He's still pretty grumpy. Wants to know why we haven't made more progress with the murder enquiry. He was pleased to hear about the two boyos in the van though," Hays said.

Lyons went on to tell Hays about Fahy's interaction with Peter Hackett.

"Do you think we should get him to do some more digging?" Lyons said.

"I'd like to, but it's going to be hard to justify. It's not as if it's on our patch, and it would be almost impossible to get any evidence that would stand up. I think perhaps the British police were right to park it. Tell you what. Why don't I pursue that end of things a bit? There was a DCI on the course that came from Northampton. Perhaps I'll give him a call and have a chat," Hays said.

"Yeah, that's a good idea. I hate to think of Weldon profiting from some serious fraud like that. It just annoys me," Lyons said.

"Karma, Maureen, karma. He'll get his, wait till you see."

John O'Connor knocked on Hays' door bringing their conversation to an end.

"Yes, John. Come in. What have you got?" Hays said, beckoning the young Garda into the office.

"Aidan Doyle, sir. Quite a character. I found him on a web site he uses to promote his services, and there's only a photo of him standing proudly beside his VW Golf van. And there's more."

"Go on, John," Hays said.

"The van's reg number is JDI 9416, so I put that into PULSE and bingo! JDI 9416 was caught on CCTV when Doyle filled the van up and left the garage without paying. He's a bad boy this one. Quite a rap sheet. ABH, burglary, vehicle theft and so on, but nothing too recent, except for the diesel thing," O'Connor said.

"Where is the petrol station?" Lyons asked.

"Loughrea. Only about 40km east of Galway. I've printed a few stills of the CCTV for you, sir."

"Great, thanks John, good work," Hays said.

Lyons studied the A4 prints that O'Connor had given them. There was a clear face picture of the man looking directly into the camera.

"Anything on Nicola Byrne Ellis at all John?" Lyons asked.

"I haven't got going on her yet, Inspector. But I will now."

"Thanks."

"Spot anything helpful?" Hays asked Lyons when O'Connor had gone scurrying off to dig up information on Doyle's partner.

"I sure do. Look at the date. Coincidence? And the time fits too." Lyons said.

"Yes. And that's the day Nicola Byrne said the two of them were tucked up in Ringsend eating a Chinese. You didn't happen to clock the name of the take-away on the corner near her house, I suppose?" Hays said.

"Of course I did. It's The Silver Orchid," she said rather indignantly.

"OK. Well here's the plan."

Chapter Twenty-three

Hays went through the small batch of cards that he had collected whilst he was attending the course in Dunstable.

"Ah, here it is," he said as he stared down at the name Richard Gibson, Detective Chief Inspector, Northamptonshire Police printed neatly on the card with a crest alongside it.

Hays dialled the number on the card, prefixed with the International code for the UK, 0044.

The phone was answered immediately.

"Gibson," the voice at the other end said.

"Ah, Richard. This is Mick Hays from Galway. I see you're back in harness already. Did you enjoy the course?" Hays said.

"Yes, yes, it was good. Very informative. You got back OK?" the man said.

"Yeah, no bother. But after I'd finished in Dunstable, I drove north to your area. Just something we're investigating over here – rather a nasty murder as it happens," Hays said.

"Really. You should have called in, we could have had a pint."

"Well, maybe next time. But there is something you might be able to do for me, Richard. Our enquiries have led us to have a look at a Jack Ashton. He runs a stable and livery operation at a place called Dale View Farm near Spratton. Any chance you could have a root around and see if you have anything on him at all? There's just a few loose ends I'd like to tidy up."

"Yes, sure. Things are fairly quiet here just now. Ashton you say? I'll have a bit of a snoop and see if there's anything. Just give me your mobile number, and I'll give you a call if I find anything."

Hays gave Richard Gibson his details and thanked him for his help.

"Oh, and before you go Richard, you might see if there's a guy called Hackett involved at all. He's an investigator for Ashton's insurance agents at Lloyds, and he may have provided some information," Hays said.

"Hackett. Right, I have that now. I'll get back to you."

* * *

The Irishtown Gardaí lifted Aidan Doyle from his house that evening. They told him that they were arresting him on suspicion of stealing €58.46 worth of diesel from an Esso petrol station in Loughrea, County Galway, and that they would be taking him to Loughrea Garda Station for questioning. He protested loudly, but the Gardaí were having none of it, and soon he was handcuffed in the back of a squad car travelling across the country in a westerly direction.

It was a dismal autumn evening as the squad car sped down the N6 with heavy grey clouds overhead and just an annoying amount of light rain falling on the windscreen. They reached Loughrea at just before nine o'clock, and Doyle was booked in and shown to a cell for the night by the desk sergeant, a man well used to dealing with criminals protesting their innocence.

When Hays and Lyons arrived the following morning, Doyle was feeling really sorry for himself, but was angry too at being carted half way across the country for the sake of fifty odd euro.

"Do you know why you're here, Mr Doyle?" Hays began.

"No, I effing don't. I ain't done nothing," he protested.

Hays said nothing but produced one of the photos John O'Connor had printed from the CCTV and placed it in front of Doyle.

"This was taken two weeks ago at the Esso station on the edge of town here. It clearly shows you putting fuel in your van, Mr Doyle."

"Yeah, so? It doesn't run on fresh air you know!"

"But it seems, Mr Doyle, that you drove off without paying for the tankful of diesel."

"That's not true. Of course I effing paid for it. Do you think I'm a fool?"

"Cash or card?" Hays asked.

"Card of course. That way I get the VAT back, don't I?"

"So, your card statement will clearly show a transaction for €58.46 on that date then, right?"

"Eh, well maybe not. I might have forgotten to pay. I was exhausted after working all day and then driving all the way out to this dump. But I'll pay for it now," Doyle said.

"What were you doing out here anyway? It's a long way from home," Lyons asked.

"I had to collect a part for an air-conditioning plant I'm working on in one of the warehouses I look after," Doyle said.

"What, at seven o'clock at night?" she said.

Doyle shuffled uneasily in his seat and looked down at the table.

"A mate of mine was going to meet me with it out at Ballybrit," Doyle said.

"Can we assume that this was not an entirely legitimate transaction then, Mr Doyle?" Hays said.

"He only wanted €300 for it, and I can rebill it at €850 plus VAT, so it was worth the trip."

"And where does this mate of yours work?" Hays said.

"ThermoPlant. He works in the warehouse."

"What's his name?"

"Jimmy. I don't know his second name."

"And did you meet this Jimmy?"

"No. He never turned up, the lousy fecker, and me after driving all this way. I drove all around looking for him, but there was no sign, so I eventually had to drive all the way back without the part. Cost me a fortune in diesel."

Hays decided not to mention that it had in fact cost him nothing in diesel as he had stolen a refill for his van.

"So, you drove straight back to Ringsend?"

"Yeah. I was going to stop at the Esso place and pay them for the diesel, but it was closed by the time I was passing."

"What time was that then?" Hays asked.

"About half-nine. I got back home at around half-twelve. Nicola was in bed," Doyle said.

"So, you admit to stealing €58.46 worth of fuel then?"

"I never meant to, honest. I'll pay for it now, no bother."

"I'm sorry, Mr Doyle, but that's not how it works. The Gardaí take fuel theft quite seriously in these parts, there's far too much of it. I want to check out a few things and then I'll be charging you. But don't worry, you'll be bailed on this occasion despite your colourful past," Hays said.

The Loughrea Gardaí had given Hays and Lyons the use of an office, and they retreated there following the interview with Doyle.

"Maureen, can you get the locals to check out a few things for me? Firstly, what time does that Esso station close up on a weekday, and in particular, what time did it close on the night in question? Then ask them to call ThermoPlant and see if they have a warehouseman called Jimmy. Oh, and could you get the boys in Irishtown to call in to The Silver Orchid when it opens and see if they have a record of an order for Nicola Byrne on the same night. I have a feeling she may be a regular customer of theirs in which case they'll probably have it in their computer," Hays said.

"Sure. What will you be up to?" Lyons said.

"I'm going to call John back in Galway, see if he's dug up anything on Nicola Byrne. It looks to me as if she's been lying to us," Hays said.

As the morning wore on, information began to flow back to Loughrea. The Chinese take-away did indeed have a record of Nicola's order on the night of the murder, but it was just dinner for one, not two, and they had delivered it the fifty metres down the road to her house. So, she had given her partner an alibi. Hays wondered why that was necessary if all he was doing was collecting some dodgy parts. As he was pondering this, one of the uniformed Garda from the Loughrea station knocked on the door.

"Excuse me, Inspector. You know you asked me to check up on what time the Esso garage closes? Well it's normally half-past midnight, and that's when they closed the night Doyle drove off without paying," he said.

"Thanks. That's very helpful," Hays said.

He went and found Lyons.

"What are we going to do with mastermind downstairs?" she asked him.

"We've no choice. We'll have to bail him till we can find out more. Charge him with the theft and then kick him out," Hays said.

"Are we going to drive him back to Dublin?" Lyons said.

"No, we bloody aren't, but I think we should arrange to interview Nicola Byrne again soon. Fancy a trip to Ringsend tomorrow?"

"Yeah, OK. But let's go early. I'll get onto Irishtown and get them to make an appointment for her to come in at around eleven," Lyons said.

"Good idea."

Chapter Twenty-four

Autumn was definitely moving in as the two detectives drove east across the country the following morning. The light had changed, and the air was cooler and fresher despite the bright sunshine.

"Funny, isn't it?" Lyons said, "as soon as the kids go back to school, after the holidays, the weather picks up."

"It does, doesn't it? I remember when I was at school and we went back the first week in September, it felt all wrong to be togged out for winter games with the sun beating down on us."

"And I bet you looked a picture in your tight little navy shorts and long socks!"

"Feck off, Lyons. I was only fourteen for God's sake!"

* * *

Nicola Byrne arrived on cue at Irishtown Garda station just before eleven o'clock. She was shown into an interview room and asked if she would like a drink of tea or water. She declined. Hays and Lyons came in carrying cardboard cups of coffee and took their seats opposite Ms Byrne.

Lyons noticed that her hair was freshly washed and hung loosely around her shoulders, and there was a whiff of some expensive perfume in the air.

"Thanks for coming in, Ms Byrne, we won't keep you long," Hays said noticing her bright blue eyes, which were locked onto him as if Lyons just wasn't there at all.

"We just wanted to go over a few things with you about the evening of the 22nd when you told us you were at home with Aidan. That wasn't strictly speaking true, was it?"

It was a moment before anyone spoke.

"Listen, Inspector, things between me and Aidan haven't been too good lately," she said, looking down at her feet.

"In what way?" Hays asked.

"Well, you've met him. He's a bit, well, rough, isn't he?"

"Go on," Hays prompted.

"When I first left David, I was very lost you see. I kind of hooked up with Aidan out of loneliness, and at that time he was kind to me. He's been in a lot of trouble with your people. And I suppose I thought I could straighten him out. And I did – to some extent at least," Byrne said.

"Do you know that he stole a tankful of diesel from a petrol station in Loughrea on the night you gave him an alibi," Lyons interjected.

"No, I didn't know that. Am I in trouble?"

"Maybe, maybe not. It depends on how things work out. You said things weren't good between you. What's going on?" Lyons said.

"Recently he's been very agitated, and he's even hit me a few times. Nothing heavy, just a few slaps really."

"Did you report it?" Lyons said.

"No. Not at all. It wasn't much. Anyway, he could have his reasons."

"Oh. How's that?" Lyons said.

Byrne shifted nervously in the chair and wrung her hands together. They waited for her to speak.

"I've been seeing someone," she eventually said, calmly.

Lyons sensed that Hays was about to tell the woman that her love life was none of their business, so she quickly gave him a little tap on the ankle under the table.

"Who have you been seeing, Nicola?" Lyons said.

"David. David Ellis. Look, I know it's crazy. After all we split up years ago. But one night a few months back after Aidan and I had a big row and he'd gone off to the pub, I called David."

"And…?"

"We met up, and got on like a house on fire. I don't know what happened, maybe it was the secrecy and naughtiness of the whole thing, but David seemed much more exciting the second time around, and he always treated me properly. He was a nice man," Byrne said. Her eyes filled with tears that ran down her cheeks.

Lyons again offered Nicola Byrne some refreshment, and this time she accepted, asking for a glass of water. Lyons looked at Hays. He got the message after a couple of seconds of apparent puzzlement, and left the room to see to the drink.

While Hays was out of the room, Lyons took the opportunity to probe a little further.

"Nicola, do you think there's any possibility Aidan could have found out about you and David?"

"I don't think so. We were very careful. We were never out together in public. I used to go to his flat in Rathgar, and once or twice we met in the cars out in County Wicklow. It sounds so seedy now as I'm telling it, but it wasn't, not at all," Byrne said.

"Does Aidan know about the life policy on David's life?"

"Yes, he does. We used to joke about how I'd be a wealthy widow when I reached eighty. 'Men always die first' he would say."

"Do you think you and David might have got back together?"

"I honestly don't know. Maybe. We'll never know now, will we?" She started to sob silently for what might have been.

* * *

At twelve o'clock, Nicola Byrne left Irishtown Garda station.

She had been put on notice that she might be charged with respect to the false alibi, but that it probably wouldn't amount to much.

"Let's get Doyle back in," Hays said when Nicola Byrne had left.

"OK. Can you arrange that? There's something I have to do," Lyons said.

"Are you going to tell me what it is?"

"You'll see. Patience, Mick, patience."

Chapter Twenty-five

It was nearly four o'clock by the time Aidan Doyle had been located and brought back to Irishtown Garda station. He was ushered into the same interview room that they had used earlier for their chat with his partner, and asked if he needed anything to drink.

"Would you like a solicitor present, Mr Doyle?" Hays asked him.

"Do I need one?"

"That's entirely up to you, but you are entitled to legal representation if you wish."

"Na, don't bother. I need to get outa here sharpish. I'm half finished a job down at the IFSC. What do ye want this time?" Doyle said.

"Tell me about your work, Mr Doyle." Lyons began when they were all seated.

"I told you before, I do maintenance for factories, warehouses and the like," Doyle said.

"Which factories and warehouses exactly?" she went on. Hays was a bit puzzled by her line of questioning, but knew her well enough to let her continue. Was Aidan Doyle about to be 'Maureen-ed?' he mused.

"There's a few places out on the Naas Road, and I have some clients in Kildare and one in Meath."

"Names, Mr Doyle, I need the names of these places," Lyons said.

"Jesus, what the hell do you want that for?" But when Lyons didn't reply, Doyle sighed heavily and went on.

"There's Zilink, Woodfords, DBL, Aero Services and Pharma Express. Look, what's all this about, Inspector?"

"What exactly do Pharma Express do, Mr Doyle?"

"They're a UK outfit with a warehouse in Ballymount. They supply stuff to independent chemists' shops and some of the bigger hospitals. Why?"

"And have you been working there recently?"

"I have as it happens. They wanted some secure storage set up for some of their more potent products with electric keypads on them, so I did that," Doyle said.

"When exactly was that?"

"Eh, end of July. What's all this about?"

Lyons tapped Hays under the table, signalling that he should take over the questioning. She excused herself from the room and went up to the open plan.

"Do you know a Mr David Ellis, Mr Doyle?" Hays said.

"Yeah, sure. Him and Nic used to be married. His loss."

"Have you ever met him?"

"No, and I don't effing want to neither. Why would I?"

"I thought you might just have come across him somewhere."

"We don't exactly move in the same circles, Inspector."

"Tell me again about your trip to Loughrea," Hays said.

"I told you already. I drove out there to meet a guy called Jimmy from ThermoPlant. He was going to liberate a control unit for me for €300. But he never showed, so I hung around for a while trying to contact him, but no luck, so then I drove home."

"That's odd. Because we contacted ThermoPlant, and they don't have a Jimmy in the warehouse – never had," Hays said.

"Well that's the name he gave me. Probably didn't want me to know his real name given the nature of the deal."

"And what time did you say that you drove back past the Esso station where you intended to pay for the fill of diesel?"

"Must have been about nine or half-past, but it was closed."

"You see, Aidan, we checked with them, and they told us that they don't close until after midnight, and they confirmed that on that particular day, they closed up at 12:35 a.m. It's recorded in their alarm system."

"I don't know, do I? It was definitely closed when I went through," Doyle said.

"So that would make it after half-twelve then. What were you doing for those three or four hours, Aidan?"

"I told you. Hanging around for Jimmy or whatever his name is."

Hays felt that without something new, he wasn't really getting anywhere, so he called a fifteen-minute comfort break and went in search of Lyons.

"Never mind," she said when he told her of the lack of progress, "Let's get back in and have another go."

* * *

Lyons restarted the interview tamely enough, going back over some of Doyle's inconsistencies. Then, out of the blue, she said, "I think on that night, Mr Doyle, you drove on out to Clifden, met David Ellis at the show grounds and killed him by lethal injection."

Hays was flabbergasted but somehow managed to keep a straight face.

"But you made one dreadful mistake," she went on, taking a plastic evidence bag out of her handbag containing a hypodermic plunger and putting it on the table.

"You left a clear fingerprint on the plunger," she said.

"I never touched it. I was wearing gloves the whole time," he blurted out.

"Where did you get that? That's nothing to do with me," he protested, trying to bluster his way past the mistake.

"Mr Doyle, a used hypodermic syringe that delivered a fatal dose of cyanide to David Ellis was recovered from a bin close to where his body was found. As you know, cyanide is a controlled substance. It took us a while, but we traced the dregs that we found in the syringe. It came from Zilink. They use it as you know in the manufacture of microchips for mobile phones. And the hypodermic originated in England. It's from a batch supplied to the Pharma Express distribution warehouse in Manchester and trans-shipped to Ireland. You have told us that you have had recent access to both of those sites, and well, what with the fingerprint, I'd say it's pretty watertight, wouldn't you?"

"Shit, shit, shit," Doyle said, burying his head in his hands.

"Right. Let's start again, shall we, Mr Doyle?" Hays said.

Over the next hour Aidan Doyle explained how he had by chance seen Nicola coming out of Ellis's apartment one day when he just happened to be driving by. After that, he followed her a few times, and it was soon clear to him that she was having an affair with him. Doyle knew about the insurance policy, and reckoned if he could take out Ellis, it would solve two problems for him. Obviously it would end the affair that Nicola was having with her ex-husband so he'd get her back, and she would then come into some real money which clearly he would help her to spend.

"How did you know where to find him?" Lyons asked.

"Easy. I got his mobile number from Nic's phone and called him. I told him I had some juicy information for him, and suggested we meet. He said he was in Clifden at the pony show, so we arranged to meet there at the show grounds at nine o'clock as my information was very sensitive, and I didn't want to be seen talking to him in a public place. The poor sap fell for it handy. The rest of it you know, but I'm positive I didn't handle the bloody needle," Doyle said.

Chapter Twenty-six

Before they left Dublin they called to Nicola Byrne's house to give her the news. She was tearful of course, but seemed to be more concerned about her own position than that of her partner.

"Are you going to arrest me too?" she asked.

"For what?" Lyons said.

"For the alibi I gave him."

"That's not up to us, Ms Byrne. But to be honest I doubt if the DPP will pursue it. We'll need to take the clothes Aidan was wearing that night, and his footwear. Could you get them for us please?" Hays said.

A few minutes later when they had Doyle's stuff secured in a large evidence sack, they left Nicola Byrne to ponder her fate.

On the way back in the car Hays asked Lyons, "How in God's name did you manage to get the syringe across from Galway so quickly?"

"I didn't. I went out and bought one in the local chemist."

"Jesus, Maureen. What about the fingerprints?"

"There isn't even one. But don't fret, I'm fairly certain we'll get a match from his clothing or footwear to the crime scene, and all the rest fits. And don't forget, he confessed, and anyway, I never said it was the same syringe!"

"Sometimes, Inspector Lyons, your methods don't exactly fit too well with police procedure, do they? Remember the cable ties from that fella O'Shaughnessy in Cork?" Hays said.

"Look, Mick. We are constrained enough by all the bloody do-gooders and bent solicitors these days. Sometimes you have to give yourself an edge, and after all, the little scum-bag is as guilty as sin."

"I just hope Plunkett doesn't get to hear of it," Hays said.

"What? You think Saint Finbarr hasn't bent the rules a few times to get a collar? Anyway, if he gets uppity we can always go after his good friend Oliver Weldon, or threaten to. That will shut him up."

"Jesus, Maureen, I hope I never get into your bad books."

"Just as long as you keep pampering me and buying me nice things and don't go off with some blonde bimbo you'll be fine," Maureen replied.

They dropped off Doyle's clothes with Sinéad Loughran on the way back to the station. As soon as they got in, Sally Fahy told Hays that the superintendent was looking for him, and he didn't sound too happy.

Hays knocked on Plunkett's door.

"Come in, Mick. Sit down. Coffee?"

"Thanks, yes please, sir."

Plunkett rang through to his secretary and asked for two coffees which were almost instantly provided along with a decent quantity of chocolate biscuits.

"So, Mick, have you made any more progress on the two thugs that assaulted Oliver Weldon?"

"They're not saying anything at all, sir. We have them banged up, and depending on whatever judge is on the bench, I reckon they'll get a couple of years apiece for ABH, but as to whatever lies behind their unprovoked attack, I don't think we're ever going to find out. But we have made an arrest in the David Ellis murder case, sir," Hays said.

Hays went on to describe the arrest of Aidan Doyle telling Plunkett that the man had confessed, carefully leaving out any reference to the syringe.

"I'm expecting a call from forensics later on to say that they can place Doyle at the scene, just to make it watertight, sir."

"Good man, Mick, well done. And did Maureen Lyons play a good part in the investigation?" Plunkett asked.

"Yes, sir, indeed she did. She was very helpful. It's really her collar you know."

"Not up to her usual tricks, I hope?"

"Perish the thought, sir." The two men exchanged a knowing look.

"Right, so, what about Weldon then?" Plunkett said.

"I don't think we should put too much more of our scarce resources into that, sir. After all, we have the two perpetrators for the assault."

"I know, but we can't just have all and sundry going around dropping upright citizens into open graves, Mick. It's not on." Plunkett said, getting a bit redder in the face.

"No, sir, of course not. But some evidence has come to light that would indicate that Oliver Weldon isn't exactly squeaky clean. He's tied up with some strange goings on with a breeder across the water – a Jack Ashton," Hays said.

"Christ, Mick, are you sure? I've known Oliver a hell of a long time and the missus plays bridge with Laura you know," Plunkett said.

"Well we probably aren't going to be able to prove anything or bring any charges. We'd need the co-operation of the British police, and to be honest, we're finding it difficult to get them to show any interest. But I'm having another go through a friend of mine in the Northampton Police."

"So, what do you suggest? I can't afford a shit storm coming down on me at this stage," Plunkett said.

"Let's leave it for a few days, and see what comes back from Northampton. Then, depending on what we find out, we could give Weldon a call. Let him know we know what he's been up to and suggest he should desist."

"Very well, Mick, but be careful now, I can hear the Aran Islands calling already!"

"Don't worry, sir."

* * *

Hays was telling Lyons about his meeting with Plunkett and they were both enjoying the story greatly, when the phone rang.

"Lyons," she said.

"Hi Maureen, it's Sinéad. Good news. We found traces of horse manure on Doyle's shoes. They match the samples we collected from the horsebox where Ellis was found, so that puts him at the scene for you."

"Excellent, Sinéad, well done and thanks," Lyons said, giving the thumbs up sign to Hays who could only hear one side of the conversation.

"That's OK," Sinéad said, "you know how much I love messing about with animal dung. Now, if only I had some roses in my window box at home, I'd be all set," she quipped.

Lyons relayed the information to Hays.

"You must be the luckiest cop in Ireland," Hays said when Lyons had hung up.

"Didn't you know, Mick? The harder you work the luckier you get!"

Chapter Twenty-seven

Hays was at his desk two days later when his phone rang.

"Hays," he said, answering the call.

"Hi, Mick. It's Richard Gibson here from Northampton."

"Oh, hi Richard. Did you get a chance to look into that thing we were talking about?" Hays said.

"I did indeed. Very interesting. Ashton came to our attention two years ago when there was an issue about the provenance of one of his horses. A local breeder made a complaint. We followed it up as best we could at the time, but with very limited resources, and more serious crimes taking place, we weren't able to pursue it to a conclusion. I spoke to the DI that handled the matter – he's not here anymore, but we still chat now and then – and he said he had concerns about the vet too – Carlyle I think his name is."

"I see. That ties in with what we have found out too. I think there's some sort of identity swap going on, and a breeder over here is involved. Is there any scope to take it further at your end, Richard?" Hays said.

"I'm not sure we can, to be honest. Tell you what. I'll have a chat with a mate of mine in the fraud squad. It's more in their line really, and maybe if you could provide them with some details of what you know, they might be able to make a move on them both."

"Yes, of course, that's not a problem. Feel free to give my details to your colleague. He can contact me anytime."

Later the same day, a man called Warren Stokes from the UK's Fraud Squad called Hays.

They talked about the case against Ashton and Carlyle for some twenty minutes, but Stokes said that unless there was some hard evidence against Ashton and Carlyle, there was little that they could do. Hays thanked the man, and hung up, feeling rather despondent.

* * *

Hays went back up to Plunkett and told him about the conversation that had taken place with the UK police.

"Well to be honest, Mick, I think it's all for the best. There's no point in us getting involved with a fairly tenuous case in the UK, even if there is Irish involvement. But if we could put an end to it without embarrassing ourselves further, it would be useful," Plunkett said.

"Why don't I give Mr Weldon a call, just to update him on progress as it were. I'll be careful not to accuse him of anything, but he'll get the message all the same," Hays said.

Plunkett gestured with an open palm to his desk phone which had an additional earpiece fitted for just such an occasion, while Hays consulted his notebook for the number.

"Mr Weldon? It's Senior Inspector Hays here. I just wanted to bring you up to date on our enquiries. How are you feeling, sir?" Hays said.

"Oh, fine thanks. It would take more than a night in a cold grave to see me off, Inspector," Weldon said, full of cheer.

"Well as you know we have the two assailants in custody now, but they're not saying anything about who was behind their attack. They appear to be frightened for their lives. But our investigations did turn up something a bit odd," Hays said.

"Oh. How so?"

"We were led to the stable yard of a Jack Ashton in Northamptonshire. I believe he's known to you?"

"Well, vaguely. I deal with a lot of UK breeders and trainers you know," Weldon said.

"Yes, but I see you've had quite extensive dealings with Ashton. Pity he has such bad luck with his animals, isn't it sir."

"What do you mean, Inspector?"

"You know three of his animals have died somewhat mysteriously recently. And there seems to be some doubt as to the provenance of some of the rest of them. There's an ongoing investigation by his insurers into it. It would be a terrible shame if somehow you got dragged into it, sir."

"I see. Yes, well thank you for letting me know. Maybe I'll steer clear of Ashtons for a bit then. And don't worry too much about the other business, I'm over it now in any case," Weldon said.

"Yes, sir, I think that would be very wise. If there are any further developments, we'll let you know," Hays said.

"Thanks, Inspector, and remember me to Superintendent Plunkett, won't you?"

"Of course, sir. Goodbye."

"Nice one, Mick. That should take care of that, well done," Plunkett said, clearly relieved that the whole business wasn't going to go any further.

"We won't have any trouble from Lyons on this one, will we?" Plunkett asked as an afterthought.

"Not at all, sir, leave that to me," Hays said.

Chapter Twenty-eight

Aidan Doyle was brought before the District Court charged with the murder of David Ellis. The judge knew Doyle well from several previous encounters and remanded him to appear in a fortnight's time at Cloverhill. He warned Doyle not to attempt to contact any witnesses, and told him that if he did so, the ultimate sentence would be increased.

Lyons phoned Mr Warner at Consolidated Life and General and informed him that they had made an arrest for the murder of David Ellis.

"I see," said Warner, "and is Mrs Ellis involved at all?"

"Only very marginally, Mr Warner. She initially gave the accused an alibi for the night that the crime was committed, but she has withdrawn it now," Lyons said.

"Hmm, nevertheless, I think that gives us sufficient grounds to decline her claim, at least initially. Can you provide us with some details, Inspector?"

"Not until the trial is over. Do you think that's a bit harsh, Mr Warner? She has no income now Ellis's alimony has stopped, and she'll probably lose her home."

"Company policy, I'm afraid, Inspector. And you know a claimant can't benefit from a crime involving the proceeds of an insurance policy. Will she be charged with aiding and abetting?" Warner said.

"Well that's not up to us, but there doesn't seem to be any evidence of actually assisting with the murder, and she may have given the alibi under duress as well, so I doubt if the DPP will proceed against her. She'll probably just get a caution."

"Pity," he said.

You're all heart, Lyons thought to herself as the conversation with the insurance company came to an end.

* * *

In the end, Nicola Byrne didn't receive the insurance money. She managed to come to an arrangement with the building society to rent her cottage from them, and after two years she met another man whom she fell in love with and who treated her properly. They eventually bought the property back from the bank, and are still living there to this day.

When Doyle got to trial, he pleaded guilty to the murder of David Ellis at the Connemara Pony Show and was given a life sentence with a recommendation that he serve at least fifteen years before being considered for parole. He was taken away to Mountjoy prison.

Oliver Weldon had been given a good fright having spent the night in an open grave. What with that and the none too subtle warning from Senior Inspector Hays, he decided to give up his shady dealings and turned his attention to regular breeding at which, it turned out, he was very successful. In any case, he had made a lot of money from the business with Ashton, so he didn't need to pursue the crooked trade.

Jack Ashton didn't fare so well. After another death at his yard that couldn't be accounted for within the bounds of reasonableness, the stable boy, Malcolm Fulton, went to the authorities and told them of his concerns. While no criminal charges were brought against Ashton, he did lose his breeder's license and had to sell up. When last heard of, he was involved in timeshare sales on the Costa Del Sol in the south of Spain.

Jenny Gillespie continued to ride Lady. It took her quite a while to get over her experiences at the pony show and although she never went back, she continued to enjoy her favourite hobby. When she was eighteen however she had a bad fall from Lady during a cross-country hack and broke her pelvis. It was a bad break, and her mobility was affected permanently, so while she didn't ride again, she continued to look after her pony, and, as she saw it, her best friend.

Tony Halpin, the amorous part-time school teacher was not prosecuted for his alleged abduction of Jenny Gillespie. Jenny wanted nothing more to do with the incident. She could imagine a courtroom scene with some sleazy barrister accusing her of coming on to Halpin, trying to make out it was all her fault, so she refused to co-operate in any prosecution.

Sergeant Mulholland was not best pleased. On his nightly visit to Cusheen's where he enjoyed a few pints before heading home, he made sure that the locals were made fully aware of Halpin's proclivities.

"And to think that the dirty pedo still has access to the town's children. It isn't right you know," he would say to the locals in the pub. The men-folk of Clifden took the cue, and on a dark and damp October evening, four of them rocked up to Halpin's house, armed with a couple of pickaxe handles and a short iron crow-bar. Halpin got a good hiding and was instructed to leave town the following day, and not to return, or next time he wouldn't be so lucky.

The next day Halpin turned up at Clifden Garda station very battered and bruised and told Sergeant Mulholland that he had been set upon and beaten up.

"I see something has happened to you, all right, Mr Halpin. Four men you say? Have you got any witnesses?" the sergeant asked.

"No, just myself."

"Right so. Did you recognize any of these men at all?"

"No, but I might if I saw them again, perhaps in a line up," Halpin said.

"Ah that's all a bit Hill Street Blues for us out here, Mr Halpin. We do things a bit differently."

Sergeant Mulholland took Tony Halpin by the arm and led him outside into the cool October day.

"You know, it gets very dark at night up where you live, Mr Halpin. I'd say what really happened is you probably tripped over something in the dark and fell down awkwardly. This tale about four men sounds very far-fetched to me," Mulholland said.

"Is that it? You're not going to do anything about it? I could report you for this you know," Halpin said incredulously.

"Mr Halpin, I've more to be doing than running after the likes of you that can't find their way around in the dark. Now away with ye and don't be bothering me with your nonsense! And as for reporting me, well good luck with that now."

Halpin had no choice. With the Gardaí unwilling to pursue the assault on him, he took heed of the warning and left Clifden for good the same day. In an unusual twist of fate, his Land Rover was insured by Consolidated Life and General, and he collected €800 for the write off of the vehicle which still lay stuck in the sand out beside the causeway leading to Omey Island. When the tide was low, you could see the top half of the rusting hulk covered in shells, where the limpets had attached themselves to it.

* * *

One chilly night in November when it was all over, Hays and Lyons were sitting at home in front of a lovely warm turf fire having a glass of red wine after dinner.

"Mick, have you any life insurance?" Lyons asked.

"What? Thinking of bumping me off now, are you?"

Lyons gave him a dig in the ribs.

"Don't be daft. But seriously, we're both in a high-risk occupation, and if either of us got killed in the line of duty, the other would have a lot of financial issues. An insurance policy – you know, I insure you and you insure me – would help, wouldn't it?"

"Well, I have a mortgage protection policy on this place, but that's about it," Hays said.

"Yeah, but if the worst happened, who gets the house. Not me, that's for sure."

"I see what you mean. Maybe we should think about it. Of course, there is another way around the issue."

"What? Oh no you don't, Mick Hays. If you're going to propose to me, it will be on a white sandy beach on a Caribbean Island with you down on one hairy knee, and a bloody great diamond in your fist."

"Well, that's me told," he said, putting his arm around her.

Maureen snuggled in close to him. Despite her rebuttal, she still felt butterflies in her stomach and a warm glow spread through her entire body, and it wasn't from the wine.

Character List

Senior Inspector Mick Hays – an experienced detective based in the Galway Detective Unit in Mill Street. Hays is unsettled, contemplating his future in the force, and with his partner Maureen Lyons.

Inspector Maureen Lyons – a sassy Detective Inspector with a great nose for clues who is not beyond pulling the occasional stunt to bring justice to bear.

Superintendent Finbarr Plunkett – a wily senior policeman with friends in all the wrong places. He has plans to expand the unit and progress his career at the same time.

Detective Sergeant Eamon Flynn – a tenacious young detective who follows every lead until he gets a result.

Detective Sally Fahy – a very bright young detective making a name for herself with the other members of the team.

Garda John O'Connor – a nerdy technophile that likes nothing more than cracking computers and mobile phones to reveal the secrets people try to hide.

Sergeant Séan Mulholland – the laid back 'member in charge' at Clifden Garda station who turns out to be more steely that anyone would give him credit for.

Garda Jim Dolan – works with Mulholland in Clifden at a gentle pace.

Sinéad Loughran – the ever-cheerful forensic team lead who uses humour to offset the gruesome nature of her work.

Pascal Brosnan – the Garda from Roundstone that runs the local station single-handed.

Darragh Clancy – a sharp eyed Garda manning a roadblock on the Donegal Road.

Dr Julian Dodd – a highly experienced pathologist who is always at hand when there's a corpse to be examined.

Jenny Gillespie – a young, attractive horse-woman who owns a Connemara pony called 'Lady'.

Cathal Gillespie – Jenny's father.

Máiréad Gillespie – Jenny's mother.

Mrs Cathleen Curley – the rotund owner of the Ocean View Guesthouse who likes to know what her guests are up to.

John Curley – Cathleen's industrious husband who is looking to extend their business.

David Ellis – the hapless victim of a brutal murder whilst investigating some funny business in the bloodstock trade.

Oliver Weldon – the somewhat snobbish head of the Connemara Pony Society who has made a great deal of money from dealing in horses, some of which may be from questionable sources.

Jack Ashton – runs a small stable yard in Northamptonshire that has had some success with racehorses, but seems to be blighted by bad luck.

Victor Carlyle – veterinary surgeon to the Ashtons' stables.

Mr Warner – the rather heartless claims manager from an insurance company.

Gregg Newman – the managing agent at a Lloyds syndicate specializing in equine insurance.

Malcolm Fulton – the talkative stable boy at the Ashtons' yard in England.

Laura Weldon – Oliver's long-suffering wife.

Mrs Magee – Cathleen Curley's home help at the Ocean View.

Nicola Byrne – David Ellis's estranged wife.

Aidan Doyle – Nicola Byrne's current partner.

If you enjoyed this book, please let others know by leaving a quick review on Amazon. Also, if you spot anything untoward in the paperback, get in touch. We strive for the best quality and appreciate reader feedback.

editor@thebookfolks.com

www.thebookfolks.com

BOOKS BY DAVID PEARSON

In this series:

Printed in Great Britain
by Amazon